T(

JOANNA BLAKE

TORPEDO

I'm Gabriel Jackson. I'm a naval officer. I love three things: my crew, my ship, and sinking my torpedo.

I thought I'd go career for life. But an injury puts me on dry land. That's when I see her for the first time in years.

Tabitha Peterson.

The girl from the wrong side of the tracks. The girl who didn't dress to impress but still caught my eye, and every other eye, in a hundred mile radius. The girl I'd done my best to catch back in the day, with zero luck.

I'd always wondered what happened to Shabby Tabby.

Now I know, because she's the aid sent to help take care of me at home. She's more tempting than ever, with her crazy curves and big, beautiful eyes. She's still got that brick wall and chip on her shoulder too. I go from being bored stiff to having the challenge of my life.

I have two missions: learn to walk again and get Tabby where I've wanted her all this time. *In my arms and in my bed.* I don't care if we do it lying down, sitting down or standing on one leg. I want to tear her walls down just as bad as I want to tear her clothes off.

I'm just not prepared for what comes after. How badly she's been hurt or how badly I want to protect her. I'll risk everything to make her mine, for good.

Torpedo is a stand alone novel with a guaranteed HEA and no cheating!

Created with **Vellum**

For my husband.

FIVE YEARS AGO

I flexed my back, waiting for my turn to run sprints. I was already warm but I never stopped moving during practice. It was a small town, and not a rich one either. We didn't have a lot of equipment so we had to take turns running drills. I didn't mind though. It gave me time to think about what I had to do *after* practice.

Tonight, I was going to get the girl I'd been dreaming about for years.

I was popular with the ladies, to say the least. Good looking and from a nice family. Decent grades and the quarterback for one of the best football teams in the state. It wasn't that I was hard up for a date. But for some reason, I'd always wanted the one girl I couldn't have.

Shouldn't have.

Girls like her and boys like me didn't mix.

But fuck that. I wanted what I wanted. And from the stares we'd exchanged over the years, I was pretty sure she liked me too.

"There she goes."

My head swiveled as a girl in faded clothes walked past the exterior fence. She looked tense, like she knew we were looking at her. Hell, she ought to be used to it by now.

Everyone was always looking at Shabby Tabby.

I winced at the name, even though I'd just heard it in my head. It wasn't nice. And it definitely didn't do her justice.

The girl might be poor, but she was the best looking girl in this town. Maybe the whole damn state. She'd been blessed with curves that could tempt a saint and the beautiful face of an angel.

I wasn't even religious.

And I definitely wasn't alone.

Everybody wanted Tabby. Guys had been trying to score with her since she hit puberty. Many claimed to have succeeded, but I had my doubts.

The girl looked too pure to me to have had mortal hands on her. Somehow, even in her threadbare clothes, she looked clean as the driven snow. It didn't change the fact that her body was made for sin.

She looked like a pin-up girl or a centerfold. On steroids.

Either way, I was finally taking a crack at her tonight.

I'd waited too long. It was halfway through senior year. If I wanted to go out with Tabitha, it was now or never.

Because once I left this town, I wasn't coming back.

Most of my friends were going to the local community college, with a few guys from the team going to state. A few weren't going to school at all, just taking jobs on fishing boats or in their family businesses like my buddy Lyle.

But me stick around this small town? Hell, no. I was joining the Navy. I was gonna see the whole damn world if I had my way about it.

I grunted, staring at the way Tabitha moved in those worn-in old jeans of hers. Most girls had twenty pairs of jeans. I was fairly certain that Tabby had two. I knew, because I kept track of everything about her. Especially anything that touched her perfect, juicy ass.

She had a dark pair and a light pair of jeans. Both fit her like a glove.

A tight glove.

Maybe a little *too* tight. But damn, that was a mighty fine thing, if you asked me. If you asked *anyone.*

Anyone male with a pulse.

Tabitha had been a pretty little girl who'd grown up to be curvier than Marilyn Monroe. Quiet and studious, but nobody noticed her grades. Big, luscious tits, a small waist and juicy hips that begged a man to grab hold of them.

Skinny girls might be in, but a woman with curves like that... well, she never went out of style.

Not with any red-blooded American male anyway.

She glanced over her shoulder before turning the corner. I could have sworn she saw me. Looked right into my eyes. I felt the start of a boner, right then and there.

Nuh uh. Not good. Down boy.

I grabbed my jock and pressed down on it, noticing that a few other guys were doing the same. Didn't matter. The team captain should not be getting a boner standing in the middle of the damn field.

Thankfully it wasn't long before the coach called practice. I hit the showers and cooled down with a blast of icy cold water before soaping off. Pretty soon I was jogging to my car, ready to get on with the weekend already. I dropped my best friend Lyle off and then ate an early dinner with Ma. I showered again, and put on a nice button down shirt. I even splashed a little aftershave on my cheeks.

Just a touch though. I didn't want to drive the girl away. I wanted her to get *close.*

As close as possible.

There was a bonfire at the beach tonight. I was hoping Tabby would be there. Hell, I was hoping she'd give me the time of day. She didn't socialize much, but everyone went to the bonfires. It wasn't just for the rich kids or the jocks or the druggies or whoever.

It was more about football than anything else, but either way, everyone turned out.

I drove down to the beach after picking up Lyle and Topher. They were already drinking. I was driving tonight so I wasn't having anything. It was better that way, especially if my plans worked out.

I didn't care about drinking with my boys. I just wanted to see her.

Fuck it, maybe she *was* easy. Hell, maybe I'd have her underneath me tonight. The image of us going at it gave me renewed energy. I put the pedal to the metal. I even cleaned out the backseat once we pulled into the parking lot just in case.

Just to be prepared…

The party was already hopping with at least three kegs on tap. I was surrounded by the popular crowd right away. Other athletes and most of the cheerleading squad were in a cluster, their chatter flowing around me like water.

I smiled and nodded and kept my eyes peeled for my quarry.

About an hour later I finally saw her. She was sitting on a piece of driftwood, half-heartedly sipping from a red cup. Another girl I saw her hanging around with sometimes was sitting beside her. Jackie. The girl had a nose ring and short dark hair.

There was a guy too. Dennis something. I wasn't worried about him though. The word was that he played for the other team.

As long as he wasn't competition, he was off my radar. I got a fresh beer and walked over to her. She looked up and our eyes met. She was wearing that beat up old army jacket of hers.

Somebody had told me it was her daddy's. I knew she lived with her grandma, so I assumed her folks were gone. The jacket swallowed her petite frame, making it hard to see her gorgeous body. Didn't matter. Her face was enough to stop traffic.

Huge, dark hazel eyes stared up at me, almost looking gold in the firelight. Her skin was a creamy, warm olive tone. Her high cheeks and full lips were pink and soft. And her cute little nose was just slightly upturned, making her look a little bit mischievous.

A lot mischievous, I hoped.

"You want a fresh beer?"

I held it out to her and she took it, then looked back at me suspiciously.

"It's not spiked. Here."

I took a sip and handed it back. She took it and had a small sip.

"Thanks."

"Mind if I sit down?"

She shrugged non-commitally. Her friends made themselves scarce and I sat next to her. She smelled amazing. Clean and fresh and girly. Not like perfume though. Just like... soap and warm skin.

I felt a surge of lust, thinking about touching that skin.

"I'm Gabe."

She rolled those gorgeous eyes at me.

"Yeah, I know. We kinda grew up together."

I cleared my throat.

"Yeah, but we never talked."

"That's true."

"Thought I'd remedy that. Before school was over for good."

She looked at me, then turned back to the fire. She wasn't making this easy. Not that she was being rude. She just wasn't falling into my lap and taking off her top either.

"So I was wondering..."

"Yeah?"

"If you'd go out with me."

Now she was looking at me.

"What do you mean?"

"We could go out. Hang out. Together."

She rolled her eyes and stood up.

"You mean roll around in the back of your car."

"What? No-"

She stood up and walked away from me. I chased her across the sand towards the water. Finally she stopped. She seemed surprised to see me behind her.

"I didn't mean it like that-" Even if I had just cleaned out the back of my car. But there was no reason for her to ever know that. I cleared my throat. "I meant we could date. Exclusively."

She chewed her lip and stared at me. I gave her a charming smile and tried to tease her.

"You know... go to the movies. Get something to eat... crazy stuff like that."

She looked almost hopeful for a second.

"Why?"

"What?"

"Why do you want to date me? Did someone tell you I was easy? Because I'm not."

"Hey, Tabitha- no- I mean-"

"Forget it, Gabe. You seem like an okay guy but- I'm not up for it. Thanks anyway."

I grabbed her arm before she could run off.

"Wait."

She gave me a hard look. She had a reputation as kind of a tough girl. I was suddenly realizing why she had to be.

"Just...Why not?"

I stared at her face in the moonlight. She was almost too pretty. I wanted to kiss her but she looked upset. I didn't get why asking her out would hurt her feelings, but I could see it had.

"Is it me?"

She looked at me and I saw something in her eyes that pierced my stupid teenage brain for a minute. Her feelings *were* hurt. She *did* think I just wanted sex. And dammit, maybe she was right.

"No Gabe. You're- just find someone who wants to roll around with you. I'm sure there are plenty of takers. Goodnight."

And then she was gone.

GABE

"Almost there, Sir."

"Don't think he can hear you."

"I read that the subconscious mind perceives everything."

"Yeah, whatever. You're just doing that because you think he's hot."

"Well, he *is* hot."

"He's an officer. You shouldn't be looking at him like a piece of meat."

"Honey, once you pierce the surface, we're <u>all</u> meat."

I opened my eyes to see two women in white standing over me. I squinted. Everything was bright. *Too bright.* The lights were shining. Everything was clean and white.

For a minute, I thought I was in heaven.

Actually, that made sense. Maybe I was gone. On the other side.

The last thing I remembered was an explosion. I had been on deck when it hit. We hadn't been expecting an attack. We weren't even in range. But the damn ship had blown up all the same.

I didn't have time to even shout out a warning when I saw the flash of light. All I did was push Donner out of the way. He'd been the only one standing nearby.

I hoped so anyway.

I wondered if we'd been hit if that meant things had escalated with Russia. We were already on a tight leash, patrolling the waters of the Black Sea on a precise schedule. We did not deviate from the route or speed.

Ever.

But we should have known if something was coming. And it hadn't seemed like a direct hit. You could usually hear those coming.

It could have been mechanical, I figured. All I saw was a bright light before the darkness. I closed my eyes. Actually, no, I remembered screaming in pain and doctors and-

Shit.

Everything came into focus. The two nurses staring down at me were definitely not angels. One of them even had a moustache. I grimaced.

This was not heaven.

Which meant... I was not dead. Which could be a good thing, or a bad thing, depending on how bad I was hurt. I could deal with just about anything. You had to mentally prepare for majorly bad shit to happen when you were on active duty.

I could handle most of that. I just wanted my parts functioning.

Basically, I was worried about my dick.

"Oh lordy, he's awake."

The nurse with the stache was staring at me. I tried to say something but my mouth was too dry. I grimaced, and quickly one of them offered me a drink. The water tasted so good. Cool and clean and delicious. At that moment, she *was* an angel. I swallowed quickly, but she pulled it away too fast.

"Uh uh, not too fast there."

I leaned back, suddenly exhausted.

"Where am I?"

"The hospital."

"I can see that. Where?"

"Virginia."

"I'm in the U.S.?"

I was surprised as hell. The last known location of my vessel was in the Black Sea. I must have been in bad shape for them to keep me knocked out long enough to travel. Even if I got flown in.

"Where's my ship? My men? Was anyone killed?"

"Hold on, Sir. We better get the doctor."

I bit my tongue, fighting down the frustration. I needed to know about my men. *Now.*

They left and I took the opportunity to look my body over. I could sit up and wiggle my toes. I said a little prayer and lifted the blankets.

I pulled up my gown and stared down at my body. I sighed in relief. There he was. My big, beautiful cock was still attached to my body. I gripped it with one hand and grinned at the sensation. I could still feel it too. I didn't expect to get hard given whatever pain meds they had me on, but I was gonna assume it still worked.

My entire left thigh was bandaged, with blood staining the white gauze. I frowned. I could wiggle my toes, sure, but could I walk?

There were some stitches on my abdomen and other leg. I saw some on my arm too. I reached up and rubbed my face, wondering if I was still good-looking. Everything was where it should be, more or less. I guessed I was pretty damn lucky after all.

I leaned back. I would need to wait for the doc to inform me what the situation was. *After* I learned about my men. I tried to remember who had been on deck with me but it was all a blur. Davis? Cain? Donnelly?

I looked around. My IV drip was only fluids, no antibiotics or morphine. So I must be in the healing phase and out of danger. I rubbed my head and winced. I must have gotten a concussion on top of everything else.

I closed my eyes and fell asleep before I got a chance to talk to the doctor.

TABBY

"Get up here... dammit!"

I fell backwards as the cat slipped out of my hands. I was trying to trim her claws. She'd been destroying what was left of the already crappy furniture I had. I'd already sold off the few pieces worth anything.

And I needed to at least have a yard sale with what was left.

If the damn cat didn't destroy it all, that might be possible.

"You are lucky I'm sentimental or you would find yourself out on your fuzzy little tush."

I rubbed my bottom, glaring at the fleabag. Petunia was on top of the credenza, hissing at me. The credenza being one of the things I hoped to sell off when I vacated this godforsaken town.

My Grandmother's taste had not been all that stylish, but she did have some nice mid-century pieces I'd unloaded online. Now I was working my way through her collection of records and figurines. She'd been a collector, but not quite a hoarder thank goodness.

The cat hissed at me again and I rolled my eyes. Sure, we argued, but the moment I sat down there would be a truce. The cat was prickly as hell, but if you held still for five minutes, she would curl up with you and start purring.

It was an uneasy alliance, but all we had was each other.

The cat had loved Gran as much as I had. I figured we were both mourning her in our own way. The cat, by being a righteous pain in my ass. Literally.

I stood up and dusted myself off. I had only a couple more months to finish cleaning this place out. There was nothing left for me here. Gran didn't own the house, and I wasn't paying rent for a place I didn't want to live.

The lease renewed right after Christmas.

So this was it. The end of an era, more of less. Clean the place up, get what I could for the knickknacks, pick a few things to take with me for the memories.

I looked at the cat and sighed.

Take with *us.*

And then we were on to greener pastures. I'd finish nursing school and get a life. A good life. In a city where no one knew me, or had any opinion of my character, or lack thereof.

Speaking of which...

It was almost time for my shift at Garrity's.

I closed my eyes, wishing for the hundredth time my uniform was a potato sack. Oh well, there was nothing I could do about it. I hopped in the shower and changed into the black skinny jeans and tight white t-shirt they had us wear. I tried to buy a size up to hide the size of my chest, but the neckline drooped. There was nothing I could do about it.

People were gonna stare. And say things. Like they always had.

I pulled my dark hair into a high ponytail, fed the cat, and headed out to work.

GABE

I stared out of the window of the medical transport vehicle. It was an ordinary van for the most part, only tricked out with all kinds of fancy-ass equipment for carrying military personnel like me.

Mobility impaired personnel.

I refused to say handicapped, though that's what I was. My thigh muscles had been completely severed, along with some tendons and ligaments. They'd sewn me up but it a was touch and go situation.

The doctors weren't sure I would heal enough to walk normally again, but I was determined to do just that. This wasn't permanent. It wasn't.

I exhaled as the streets outside started to look familiar.

I was going back to the one place I never thought I would, other than for Christmas and Thanksgiving. The place I'd sworn to never get stuck in.

I was going home.

I hadn't seen my mom in over a year, since before I shipped out. I had most of my stuff in storage, like usual. I think it got shipped back here but I didn't know for sure.

And now I was here to recuperate. If I could. If not, well, I was going to find a high-rise condo with elevators and shit. Someplace warmer than Massachusettes.

All I knew was I wasn't staying here long.

And I sure as shit wasn't moving in with my mom for good.

No matter how much I loved her, I was a grown-ass man. This was temporary. She was welcome to move down the coast when I did to be closer. But for now, I knew I should be grateful to have family to take care of me.

The van pulled down our street and stopped in front of a tidy split-level house. My mom was standing out front. Even though I wasn't glad to be here, especially under the circumstances, I was always happy as hell to see her.

My mother was an amazing woman.

I wasn't surprised to see that her eyes were dry. I had a feeling my mom was the only lady whose son got delivered in one of these trucks who didn't shed a tear. She might cry later, and I'm sure she did when she heard I got injured, but now- dry as a bone.

My mother was a certified badass. She never showed her cards or lost her cool. She'd raised me to do the same.

And damn if I didn't love the heck out of her for it.

My dad had split when I was just a kid. But my mom didn't roll over and play dead. She worked her ass off and kept a roof over our head. She came from an upper middle-class family but she didn't get help from her daddy to raise me. She just buckled down and got her real estate license. Then she hauled ass.

And she *still* belonged to the PTA, a knitting circle, the lady's golf team at the local country club, even the town beautification committee.

Yeah, if you ever wanted to see a badass in a pink cardigan and pearls, look no further.

She kissed my cheek as they rolled me down the path, then directed them around back. I hadn't given much thought about where I would be staying, but this was kind of perfect. The lower level den and bedroom had been my chill out spot in high school. It had a walk-out patio and a path to the street that was wide enough for the wheelchair.

It even had a huge-ass shower and a small infrared sauna room, something my mom splurged on when her arthritis had kicked in a couple of years ago.

I looked around the place. Yeah, it was stuck in the 90's but it was still kind of cool. Mom had good taste, so even though it was dated, it wasn't too much. A comfy leather sectional and lazy boy sat over a patterned rug. The bar in one corner had matching brown leather stools.

I realized that the ottomans were all gone, and there were no stacks of magazines or firewood. She must have moved out anything that would be hard to wheel around.

The wood panelling was left over from the 1960's, way before my parents had even met. It was pretty much wall-to-wall brown, though it looked like she'd gotten a bunch of potted plants. I nodded appreciatively. It was a haven for me and my friends when we were younger.

And now, it was home.

My mom didn't hover over me, thankfully, though I did notice a pitcher of lemonade and a glass on the table. I smiled, shaking my head. It wasn't even hot out. But I did love my mother's lemonade.

One thing I would not miss about the service was the chow.

I wheeled down the hallway and looked around.

The bed was turned down and there were clean, fluffy towels at the foot of the bed too. Not that I could shower without help.

Not yet, anyway.

"Do you want visitors? Lyle's been stopping by."

I snorted. My best friend from high school had never left town, though he had visited me on base a couple of times. Even when I was stationed in Japan.

"I bet he has."

She shook her head.

"That boy has always looked up to you."

"I know. I'm sure I'll see him soon."

She nodded and I noticed she was clasping her hands together tightly.

"Dinner's at seven. I have someone coming here starting tomorrow to help out when I'm at work. An aid."

I thanked her and told her she didn't have to do that. She said she needed the help and that the military was paying for home assistance anyway. I knew she meant that I needed the help, but she spared my pride and didn't mention it.

I had a doctor appointment and my first physical therapy session in two weeks. Until then, it was just rest and recoperation.

"Thanks mom."

She handed me a bell and I looked at her, a question in my eyes.

"If you need me, just ring."

TABBY

I poured shower gel into the clean bathroom sink, using it to wash my bra and t-shirt. I didn't have time to do a full load of laundry and my work clothes all smelled like beer, even my underthings. The warm vanilla scent of my shower gel was better than dish soap for covering it up.

Plus, that's all I had on hand.

Use what you got, Grannie always said.

I smiled and shook my head. She always gave me the side eye when I called her Grannie. I only did it to tease her though.

She didn't really mind it so much anyway.

I sighed and rinsed my clothes, hanging them in the shower. I had a handful of bras and only two white t-shirts for work. If I ruined one, I was in trouble. I needed every penny to get the hell out of Dodge.

Thankfully, I'd finally gotten a call from the agency about daytime work.

Starting tomorrow, I was going to be a home caregiver.

I dried my hands and stared into the mirror, looking for answers. I made a face at my reflection. It was a nice enough face. Kind of plain, other than my eyes. And my lips, apparently.

I'd heard some guys call them blowjob lips, which made me pinch them flat as I could whenever I remembered. It had made me nauseous to realize what they were implying.

This town was full of small-minded perverts. I'd learned that when I got out and went to school. The comments had still been there, and the stares, but it was down to a minimum. Then Grannie got sick and I'd had to drop out and come home to take care of her.

Now she was gone and I was stuck here.

But it was almost over. I wasn't going to be Shabby Tabby much longer. I could go somewhere else. Be someone new.

Not the girl with second hand clothes and the body of a thirty-year-old woman at fifteen. Not the girl all the boys whispered about. And lied about. And grabbed at.

Grabbed *without* asking.

Well, that wasn't completely true. There was one who had asked. And I'd said no. Of course, it had to be the one guy I'd had a crush on forever. If he had asked me any other time, or if he'd been a little less obvious about what he was after... I might have said yes.

That was a lie. Any of my few friends could have told you I would have jumped at the chance to go out with Gabriel Jackson. He was pretty much perfect.

He was the most popular guy in school, but it was more than that.

He was gorgeous, of course, with dark hair and green gray eyes. Big and strong and agile. He'd been the best athlete the town had seen in a decade. And one of the few guys around who did not act like a total pig.

He'd even asked me out that one time. He'd been kind of sweet about it too. But I knew he just wanted to bang. Little did he know, he was casually asking for my V card.

I shook my head. That was a long time ago. Even if I'd changed my mind fifty times over the next few months, or even that summer after senior year, he was long gone. He'd done what I wanted to. Left town and never looked back.

And I was still stuck holding my damn V card.

I made myself a cup of chamomile tea and curled up on the couch with the mangy old cat.

GABE

"God dammit!"

I cursed as I tried to reach my toothbrush, only managing to knock it further away. Everything was out of reach from the chair. I stood on my good leg and grabbed the toothbrush, sitting back into the chair with a thud.

I brushed my teeth angrily, annoyed by the complexity of doing even the simplest of things. I rinsed and spat and then carefully stood and put my toothbrush back where it belonged. I scowled in the mirror before plopping back down again.

Stupid. This was so stupid. I knew there were worse things. It was not worth getting upset about.

But every damn thing was harder to do.

Just putting my pants on without hurting my injured leg required me to lay on my side. I knew the wound was healing and it would get easier. But it was frustrating as hell.

Especially since this was one thing I couldn't use my strength to solve. For this, I needed patience.

I shook my head. I'd figure out a way to make do. And I would find a way to walk again.

Until then, I was mounting a shelf in the bathroom. And bars so I could lift myself using my upper body strength. And getting a damn seat for the shower.

I would not be a whiney-ass victim dammit.

I growled as I knocked the bar of soap into the toilet.

Well, maybe I would whine a little.

I combed my hair without looking and wheeled back into the bedroom to finish getting dressed. My luggage was on a rack by the window and I could easily access it from where I was. My mother had unpacked my dress clothes but I'd shooed her off when she tried to take care of the rest.

Stack by stack I unloaded it. I put a pile on my lap and wheeled over to the dresser and back again. I did it about twenty times until my all shit was stowed. Then I zipped up the suitcase and slung it down, pushing it under the bed. It wasn't the most graceful maneuver but hell, it got the job done.

Mom had brought down a coffee machine earlier that morning and it was already percolating. She'd also left me a plate of eggs and fruit. I grumbled a bit about the lack of bacon, but I had a feeling mom was not going to budge on a healthy diet. She'd already given me an earful last night over dinner.

I wolfed down the eggs and coffee and realized I didn't have to rush for once in my life. In fact, I didn't have one damn thing to do with myself. I looked around. There was plenty of stuff I could fix in here. Things to help mom out the way I did every time I came home for a holiday.

I could paint the place. Repair the side table that was leaning to one side. The back patio had some bricks coming up from the soft, loamy ground we had out here. But none of that was happening while I was in the chair.

I rolled my shoulders and decided to get to work on the one thing I could control at the moment.

My recovery.

If I kept the rest of my body in good working order, then maybe my leg would heal faster. Or at least I would not go out of my freaking mind.

I eyed the sofa and the edge of the fireplace. Deciding the fireplace was more manly, I scooted my body from the chair onto the lip and started doing dips. I eased down onto my knees and turned around to do push ups on the floor, keeping the weight off my bad leg.

I was pretty sure the physical therapy folks would frown on this, seeing as my stitches were barely out, but damned if I was going to go soft. I did two sets of fifty, alternating dips and pushups. I was just finishing up the second set when I heard footsteps on the stairs.

I counted out the last few reps and turned over, sitting on the floor with my back against the fireplace. There, if I could do that a few times a day, plus crunches, I would not be getting soft. I just had to watch my injury and go slow.

At least it was something.

I wiped the back of my wrist over my forehead as mom came down with my new aid. I froze with my hand still over my forehead and stared. I could hardly believe my eyes.

Dark hair, big hazel eyes and curves that wouldn't quit. A beautiful mirage from my teenage fantasies. The girl who had haunted my dreams all those years ago.

My new aid had just walked into the room, looking just as shocked as I did.

And a damn sight less happy.

I was grinning ear to ear, but she sure wasn't.

A gorgeous brunette stood in front of me, tight jeans casing long, impossibly curvy legs. And good lord, that was just her legs. Her long hair was pulled back in a ponytail that made her look like a schoolgirl. She was wearing a plain button down shirt that did little to disguise her ridiculously sexy body. There was no mistaking the Jessica Rabbit proportions of the girl who'd driven me crazy throughout all of high school.

Fuck it. Junior high too.

Tabitha fucking Peterson.

This was amazing. Awesome. Fantastic.

And a total fucking disaster.

This girl- scratch that- this woman- had done more than haunt my horny teenage dreams. I'd still thought of her over the years. Searched for her now and then online with no luck. I only had my memories and a few pictures in the yearbook to remember her by.

She looked even better now, if that was even possible.

So yeah, I was glad to see her. More than glad. I felt like an old house that had the power turned back on. A busted car with a new battery.

But my pride was rearing its ugly head.

Tabitha was the last damn person I wanted seeing me like this. I wanted to screw her brains out, not have her wipe my ass. Not that it had come to that but- well, fuck it. It was the principle of the matter.

I frowned. She looked even less psyched than I did. That surprised me. Everybody else was acting like I was a war hero, even if the accident had been a equipment malfunction. She didn't know that. Hell, I'd just found out the barest details myself.

The Navy was notoriously tight lipped when shit went wrong. Which it had, rather spectacularly. I'd finally heard from the guys last night. I'd known that no one was killed in the explosion. Johnson got a mild concussion with some hearing loss and I got clipped, but that was it. Davis and Cain hadn't even been above deck.

Two of us, out of the service. But everyone had survived. Even the ship was being refurbished, though the guys had been reassigned.

We were fucking lucky.

Right now though, I didn't feel fucking lucky.

"You two know each other, don't you?"

I nodded curtly. Tabitha said nothing. I noticed the way her neatly pressed shirt was fraying at the edges, the plain straight lines of it doing nothing to distract from her outrageous figure. Her eyes were dark as she looked me over.

"Do you need help getting into the chair?"

"No, I'm good, thanks."

"On the floor?"

"Yes. I'm good. On the floor."

I smiled at her pleasantly. I had to figure out how to get her to leave, and then come back when I could walk and let me take another crack at her. And I meant to take another crack, and then some.

"Mom, can I talk to you alone?"

Tabitha didn't wait to be asked. She stalked over to the patio door and out. I did my best not to stare at that ass of hers. It had been way too long since I got laid, I realized. That was the only way to explain the way my body was reacting.

Because I was close to being fully hard and my mother was in the damn room.

"Yes?"

"Mom, this isn't going to work. First of all, she's not strong enough to lift me."

"She is, actually. They have to pass a test."

I clenched my jaw and ignored that little tidbit.

"And second of all, I don't need a damn babysitter. I just need a little help now and then and a nurse to change the dressing. That's it."

"Well, Tabitha *is* a nurse."

My jaw dropped at that.

"She is?"

"I believe she had one year of nursing school. She came home to take care of her grandmother. She's actually more qualified than most home aids. Unless you want a visiting nurse service and that's a much more expensive proposition. The doctor didn't think you needed it."

"I don't need a twenty-four hour nurse. I don't need anything-"

"Tabitha knows how to follow the doctor's instructions and help speed your recovery. You want that, don't you?"

I clenched my jaw.

"She's a very nice young lady. I knew her grandmother."

She gave me a look that could freeze boiling water.

"I hope you haven't treated her unkindly, Gabe. I know how snobby people in this town can be. I didn't raise you to judge people because they don't have money."

"No. I don't. I haven't."

"Good. I'll just tell her to come back in so I can get to the office. Unless there's something else?"

I knew I'd been beat. My mom couldn't stay here all day and she wasn't willing to leave me alone. I'd just have to set this place up so I could be here by myself. This wouldn't last more than a week or two.

I was sure I'd be walking again in a month anyway. I had to be.

Tabitha came back in and hung her purse on the back of a chair. I decided to use this time to get to know her. To find out if she had a boyfriend. Hell, maybe I'd have a real shot at her now.

"So."

"So."

She pulled out a pad and a pen.

"What would you like for lunch? Any food allergies?"

"Are you going to write everything down?"

I was grinning but she just stared at me.

"Yes."

"Come on, Tabitha. Tell me how you've been. It's been a long time."

She put her arms down and bit her lip. I realized with a start that Tabitha Peterson was shy. All those years of people calling her a brazen hussy, and she looked nervous just answering a few questions about herself.

I'm not sure why exactly, but it was fucking adorable.

Plus, I actually wanted to know.

"My mom said you went to nursing school."

She nodded and cleared her throat.

"Yeah. I'm going to go back and finish. I just need to wrap up some stuff here."

"And you are a home aid now?"

She lifted her chin and stared at me defensively. Like I was interrogating her instead of trying to get her to loosen up. I'd like to help relax her- starting with getting her out of her clothes.

"I'm a waitress. It's the first time the service has called me."

"So, I'm the guinea pig, huh?"

She picked up her pad again.

"Let me know what you want to eat. The notes in your file said high protein and lots of vegetables. And it's almost time for your meds."

I leaned my head back and exhaled.

"I'm not picky. Surprise me."

She nodded and tucked her little pad into her back pocket. I perked up a bit at that, having a good view of her lower half from my seat on the floor.

"I think you should get back into the chair now. Let me help you."

"No, I've got it."

I used my arms to get myself back onto the fireplace ledge and reached for the chair. She held the handles while I scooted into it.

"You should put the brakes on next time."

I looked over my shoulder at her.

"Right. Okay, thanks."

She left to get my pills and set a timer on her phone. I stared out the window where I could see a sliver of the ocean. I used to love running on the beach, sailing and even surfing. The water looked rough today. I'd kill to be out there though.

I had a feeling today was going to be a lot less calm than the sea.

TABBY

"Try and drink one glass an hour."

He grimaced and held up his cup.

"Of juice? Can't I have a beer or something?"

I shook my head, feeling like I was talking to a child. A big, hunky child, but a child. I refilled his glass with OJ.

"Water is fine. You have to ask the doctor about beer. It might be okay if you skip your pain meds, but taken together it can be dangerous."

He moaned.

"When an American man can't even sip a beer..."

I shook my head at his dramatics.

"I'm sure you will be back in beer in no time. How is the pain today, on a scale from one to ten?"

He frowned, looking away. I could tell he was sensitive about his injury. It made sense. The most active people usually made the worst patients.

And Gabriel Jackson was more than 'active'. He was a war hero. And he'd been an incredible athlete, even as a kid.

"I need to know so I can give you your pain meds."

"I don't *have* to take them?"

I perched on the edge of the couch. It was the first time I'd sat down since I got here. I didn't know why but I was showing off a little. In full on nurse mode.

Maybe because I was afraid to let down my guard.

In fact, if I'd known who I was going to be looking after, I might have worn a potato sack. Or a suit of armor. Yeah, Gabe had wandering eyes. He always had around me.

That, at least, hadn't changed a bit. But I wasn't a starry-eyed girl who was begging for a scrap of affection anymore. I didn't tolerate anyone treating me like I was a piece of meat either.

I sat up as straight as I could, trying to project a serious vibe.

"I know it sounds macho to soldier through your pain, but it's not. If things aren't hurting so bad, we can cut your dose in half. But suffering for no reason can actually make you worse."

"It can?"

I nodded.

"Pain causes a chemical reaction in your body. Stress hormones, all kinds of things. And there's no need for it. You aren't going to get addicted."

"How do you know?"

I smiled at him without meaning to.

"It's a sign of weakness. From what I remember, that's not your thing."

A smiled transformed his face. He looked like I'd just told him he'd won the lottery, instead of giving him an accidental compliment. I stood up to hide my discomfiture.

Why the hell had I just said that? I didn't want him to know I'd noticed him all those years ago. Noticed... hell, I'd had a raging crush on him.

Too bad he'd been such an oaf when he finally made a pass at me. If he'd asked any other time, I would have said yes.

I sighed and headed for the stairs.

"Finish the juice, I'll be right back with lunch."

"Okay, Nurse Rachette."

I stopped on the first step and looked over my shoulder at him.

"I'm not a nurse yet."

"You will be."

"How do you know?"

"You aren't into signs of weakness. Not your thing."

I stared at him, realizing he was right. And he was throwing my own words back at me. And letting me know he'd noticed me too.

This felt way too personal suddenly. I was just here to provide support and that was it.

He winked and I realized I was standing there like a fool.

I forced my legs to move. I hustled up the stairs, determined to ignore Gabe Jackson, no matter what it took.

GABE

"Hmmfff, this is good."

I grinned at the gorgeous girl who was staring out the window. She was trying not to look at me, I realized. To give me privacy so I could eat.

It was considerate.

But I didn't like it.

Not one bit.

And this sandwich *was* damn good. Delicious even. She'd done something with basic turkey and made it delicious. Avocado, tomato and sliced onions. A touch of mustard and... I think she'd put a little salt and vinegar on the veggies.

I smacked my lips.

Yep, that was it. Oil and vinegar. That's the kind of sandwich you got in an authentic Italian cafe. I looked at her with newfound respect. Tabitha was full of surprises.

The girl could *cook.*

I let my eyes travel over her curves, wondering what else she could do. That led to a couple of visual images that were definitely not PG. Or even PG 13. More like R verging on those soft-core movies they showed late at night on certain cable channels.

The 'movies' with the terrible actors and actresses with fake boobs. There was nothing fake on Tabitha though. I licked my lips, looking her over.

Hmmmfff... not one damn thing. I tilted my head to the side, trying to imagine her naked. And smiling. And-

"Are you okay?"

Tabitha ran across the room and thwaked me on the back. I coughed out the bite I'd been slowly chewing. I had not been choking. I had simply been distracted by her bodacious-

"Gabe!"

She was staring at me, reaching for my mouth. I realized she was going to start manually clearing my air pipe in about three seconds if I didn't say anything. I guess she was a pretty good nurse after all. Or nurse-in-training.

"I'm fine!"

I was, however, hard as a rock. Tabby was kneeling between my knees, her hands on my thighs. It was an almost-about-to-give-head position. I stared at her, my eyes devouring her. I wanted to remember this moment, for later.

She smelled so good, like vanilla and cinnamon. She looked even better than she smelled, with her wide eyes and creamy skin, those gorgeous lips of hers parted unconsciously. It was too much. I felt my cock lurch in response.

I moaned. Loudly.

She leaned back, moving her hands away from my knees.

"Did I hurt you?"

"No. I just-"

I grabbed a magazine and dropped it on my lap.

"I'm fine."

She looked at me suspiciously, as if she knew I was lying. Or kind of lying. I *was* fine other than having a nuclear warhead in my pants. But she knew something was up.

Clearly, Tabitha's bullshit-o-meter was a finely tuned piece of equipment.

That didn't surprise me actually. She hadn't had an easy time of it back in high school. From what I could tell, the guys were always after her but she didn't have a lot of friends.

She had a reputation as kind of a tough girl actually.

She didn't look tough to me though. She never had. She looked... just over it. The girl was not easily impressed. I realized we had that in common.

"So, what *have* you been up to? Since high school?"

She narrowed her eyes at me. I could see her chewing the inside of her cheek. It made me want to yank her down on my lap and-

"This isn't a social call, Gabe. I'm here to take care of you."

I held up my hands and smiled cajolingly. Thankfully the magazine didn't slip. That would have been embarrassing.

And it would have ruined the plans I was making. My dirty mind was very, very busy today. First, I had plans to get her in bed, and then I had lots of ideas what to do once I had her there.

My earlier resistance to having her as my aid was rapidly fading. No, I did not want this ridiculously hot woman seeing me like this. But maybe I could use it to my advantage.

Gain her sympathy and all that.

Besides, I never backed away from a challenge.

Somehow, having her resist my attempts to draw her out was making me even more determined. She couldn't be more appealing if she was covered in whipped cream with cherries on top.

But she wasn't making it easy. Tabby was a tough nut to crack. I could not stop myself from wanting to crack her shell wide open.

As annoying as it was to be stuck in a wheelchair, I was going to use whatever I could to get Tabby in my bed. I was going to get this girl, once and for all. Not just once or twice either. I wanted a year long fuck-a-thon. Maybe longer.

I'd have to soften her up first though. I smiled to myself, thinking that wouldn't be a problem. I knew how to charm someone when I needed to.

By the time I was walking, she'd be at my beck and call.

"But I need to stay in good spirits. Isn't that part of healing? I thought I read that fifty percent of all healing was mental."

I gave her a sad look.

"I'm... lonely. Stuck down here by myself. I'm just asking you to talk, not for your hand in marriage."

She stared at me, her eyes searching. She glanced at her watch. Then she shrugged.

"Okay, fine. You don't need to take any pills for a few more hours. What do you want to talk about?"

I leaned back in my seat, mentally rubbing my hands together. And then undressing her. And then-

"I wondered what happened to you after high school. Fill me in."

She looked more than a little uncomfortable, but I didn't care. I was curious. And it wasn't like I was going to tell anyone.

"What do you want to know?"

I smiled.

"Everything."

TABBY

I stared at the sliver of ocean that was visible through the sliding glass doors. It must have been nice to grow up in a house like this. The rec room alone was nicer than anything at Gran's place.

"So you went to nursing school... after college?"

I nodded, trying not to look at him.

"Yes. I got an associates degree. I didn't want to do the whole four years and then get my license."

"That's smart. You're well-rounded."

He was smiling at me, with a self-satisfied look on his face. I didn't even look, but I could feel his grin. I hated this. I hated being poked and prodded. I'd told him to keep away for a reason the one night he'd spoken to me.

The night he'd basically asked me to bang.

I sighed, rubbing my arms. I looked at his impossibly handsome face, realizing he'd think it was bizarre if I ignored him completely. Even with everything he'd been through, he looked gorgeous. His dark hair and chiseled face... those eyes that were kind and mischievous at the same time.

The damn things twinkled for God's sake. And his lashes were longer than a girls! And his lips were soft and manly at the same time. The man was perfectly formed from head to toe, even with his injury.

It just was not fair how some people got dealt the best hands.

Just objectively, he was too good-looking for his own good. Or mine.

Not that I cared about things like that.

"Did you want something more to eat?"

He gave me a pointed look.

"You didn't answer my questions."

"Yes, I did."

"No, I asked how you've been. What you've been up to. You didn't even tell me if you had a boyfriend or-"

I stood up abruptly.

"I've been fine. I should check the bathroom, to see if you have enough leverage. Did you install safety equipment yet? I can help with that."

I realized I was babbling and snapped my mouth shut. Gabe was staring at me like I was a bug under a microscope. Some sort of strange creature.

I'm sure to him, I was.

I sighed and took the coward's way out.

"Why don't you take a nap?"

He stared at me, looking annoyed. Then he smiled. I wanted to tell him to stop being so charming dammit.

"But I'm not tired."

"I'll rub your back for you. Actually, I'm supposed to massage your legs but I want to check in with your physical therapist first."

He actually looked shocked.

"You're going to- rub my legs?"

"Yes. Medical massage. It speeds healing, increases blood flow, etc."

His face was pale. I think I actually saw him gulp.

I smiled grimly, determined to get him into that bed and resting until it was time to eat again. If I didn't have to look at him, or talk to him, I'd be fine.

I could maintain my hard outer shell, and my equilibrium.

"Come on, I'll just do your back for now. It will knock you right out, I promise."

He nodded and pulled himself into the chair. I watched carefully, not offering to help unless he really needed it. I knew already that wouldn't go down well.

He was stubborn as a mule. And proud. And, well, strong enough to manage most moves, as long as he stayed off his leg. His upper body was almost ridiculously thick with muscles. He wheeled himself towards his bedroom so fast I was left behind.

I noticed he had brought his magazine with him, carefully placing it on his lap.

That's weird.

I grabbed the magnesium oil I'd brought with me and followed him into his bedroom. He was already facedown on the bed when I came in. He looked over his shoulder at me.

"Shirt on or off?"

"Off is better but it's up to you."

He gave me an odd smile and pulled his shirt up and over his head. I stared, the spray bottle forgotten in my hand. He was... perfect.

His broad back was wide and carved with defined muscles. He had scars too- which only made him look more manly I thought. He wasn't a gym rat. This was a soldier's body.

Gabe was a lean, mean, fighting machine. My hands literally were itching to reach out and touch that perfection. Feel his soft looking skin, touch his meaty shoulders... his back... maybe the top of his absolutely perfect ass which was almost visible where his jeans had slipped a bit.

Pervert.

This was wrong. So, so wrong. He was a patient! The man was injured and he needed my care. I should *not* be ogling him.

Even though he seemed to just love ogling me.

I pulled myself together and sat on the edge of the bed. I poured the oil onto my hands and exhaled deeply. Be professional T. You can do it.

I rested my hands on his shoulders, shocked at the thrill that went through me at the feel of his skin.

When was the last time I had touched anyone? Or hugged them? I still talked to Jackie and Den, but they were both far away. Jackie lived in Paris of all places, and Dennis was in Jacksonville. Gran and I had hugged plenty, but she was gone.

I was completely alone, and had been for a while now.

If I wondered from time to time if I was starved for human affection.. well, this proved it. I was. This was a simple backrub. It was no reason to get all... goosebumpy about it.

I closed my eyes and pretended he was an old man. No- an old *woman.* Anyone but Gabe Jackson, spread out in front of me like a man buffet.

Focus Tabby.

Just... *rub.*

GABE

The woman was trying to kill me.

I was stretched out on the bed while Tabitha rubbed the soreness out of my muscles. I had tension I didn't even know about until she found it. It felt good. Too good.

I was afraid I was going to come all over the damn sheets.

As long as she didn't ask me to roll over... *maybe* I could try to enjoy this.

I tried to relax as her hands kneaded my shoulders. Hmmffff... her hands were strong and silky. Pleasantly cool. I felt hot everywhere they touched me though.

I imagined them slipping around to my stomach and lower, gripping my cock. In my fantasy, she wanted me as much as I wanted her. She'd bite my shoulder as she stroked me until I was close. Then she'd lift her hands away. She'd make me wait.

Not *too* long though.

She would turn me over and strip her clothes off slowly, letting me grab her glorious breasts as she straddled me and-

I stifled a moan as her hands slipped to my lower back. My cock ground into the bed. Thank the good lord for pillow top mattresses...

I rocked my hips, a little, desperate to come. How the fuck had that happened? A hard on was one thing, though

I hadn't had so much as a semi in public since I was a teenager.

But I was ready to pop, just from her hands on my back.

My fucking back.

Not my cock.

I squeezed my eyes shut and tried to think about kittens. And nuns. And nuns holding kittens.

The nuns were rubbing the kittens' soft little bellies and one of them looked like Tabby. The Tabby nun smiled at me and lifted her habit revealing her long silky legs-

I snapped my eyes open.

Nope. That was not helping. I could not block out the sweet vanilla scent of her, or how her long hair brushed over my skin as she leaned over me. The outside of her hip pressed against mine. It was so good, I had a feeling I was going to come in my pants.

And that had never *ever* happened to me before.

"Hmmfff..."

Her hands stilled immediately.

"Is that too hard?"

Yes honey, my cock is rock hard.

"No."

"Okay, good. It's especially important when I work on your leg that you tell me if it hurts. We'll go slow, don't worry."

"My leg?"

My voice almost cracked.

"Your thigh."

This time I did moan, and it definitely sounded like a sex noise. She stopped again, her voice sounding suspicious.

"Are you sure I'm not hurting you?"

Fuck yes you are hurting me. Wrap those pretty little hands around my cock instead for the love of God.

"No- I'm fine. You were right, I'm ready for a nap."

"Do you want me to bring in a drink?"

"I think I'll just sleep a little. If that's alright."

"Of course."

She stood up and I fought the urge to call her back, flip her on the bed and screw her into the mattress. She might not like the caveman approach. Then again, she might.

I knew I sure as shit would.

For now though, my imagination would have to do.

She shut the door behind her and I reached for my cock.

TABBY

I added filtered water to the soup I was making. Leftover chicken and veggies, with lots of dill and freshly ground pepper. My patient needed healthy, soothing food.

Never mind that something about him made me <u>want</u> to take care of him.

It smelled so good, I was tempted to have a bowl myself.

The kitchen was so warm and homey, with faded green and white gingham curtains and matching dishtowels and potholders. The white cabinets and tiles matched the marble countertop. It wasn't super fancy, and had little nicks from being used. But it was the nicest kitchen I'd ever cooked in.

I tried to imagine growing up here. Eating breakfast, or dinner. Doing my homework in this spot while my mother cooked a healthy supper. It must have been nice.

Not that Gran hadn't done her best. But still, I never stopped missing my mom, even though I barely remembered her.

I heard a noise downstairs and ran down to check on Gabe. He was just coming out of the bathroom. He'd changed his clothes and his hair was wet.

"Hi."

He gave me a lopsided grin. There was something absolutely endearing about it, like a little boy reveling in the act of being naughty. He looked just like a kid caught with his hand in the cookie jar.

"Hi."

"Did you shower? I need to help you with that."

"You want to help me with showering?"

He looked thrilled with the idea. I crossed my arms and shook my head at him.

"I would help you get into position on the shower stool and then wait outside. You would be- um- covered up until I left."

"Oh."

Was I crazy, or did he look disappointed?

"Well, I just splashed water on my head anyway."

I nodded.

"Good. I know it's annoying but you really shouldn't try anything like getting in and out of the shower without help."

I gave him an apologetic look.

"Not yet, anyway. Okay?"

He nodded and I sighed at the dejected look on his face. He really was like a big kid in some ways. He was surprisingly more emotional than I'd thought back in high school. I guess I'd seen him as indestructible- someone who had it all together.

It was weird seeing him vulnerable like this. And it wasn't just the injury either.

There was something.... sweet about Gabe Jackson I'd never noticed before.

Probably because he'd made me so damn nervous that I'd spent my time running away. I'd been busy ignoring the overwhelming mutual attraction between us. I'd avoided him from the first day I saw him watching me from a distance.

His eyes had been burning into me ever since, way too intensely for just a schoolyard crush.

He had been the golden boy, perfect in every way.

Handsome. Tall. Nice. A jock but not a bully. Popular but not on purpose. Smart enough but not a nerd.

And he'd never been mean to anyone as far as I could tell.

I sighed, forcing myself back to the present.

"Did you sleep?"

His cheeks went bright red. I stared, pretty sure Gabe was blushing. I rushed forward, pressing the back of my hand to his cheek.

"You're flushed! Do you have a fever?"

He stared up at me and I froze, still touching him. I had a crazy impulse to run my fingers along his jaw. To really touch him. Maybe even... kiss him.

Lord knows what he was thinking. Probably that I was crazy. But he wasn't looking at me like I was nuts. More like... he wanted to kiss me too.

His voice was husky when he replied.

"I'm fine. And yes, I, um, slept a little."

He kept staring at me and I pulled my hand back belatedly, feeling foolish.

"Thanks for the rub, by the way. My back feels great."

I nodded and turned away, trying to look busy.

"Good. I'll bring down your soup in a minute and then you can take your pills."

"Sounds good."

"Be right back."

I ran upstairs and checked the soup. It was still simmering nicely. I turned the gas off and moved the pot to an unused burner. I found a deep soup bowl and ladled some soup in, squeezing some fresh lemon juice on top.

"Oh, you're still here. Hi Tabitha."

"Hi Mrs. Jackson."

She smiled at me, looking tired. She waved me off.

"It's Ms."

"Got it."

I smiled. I'd always liked her. She always said hello when she saw me in town. And she'd served with Gran on some committee or other once upon a time.

Gabe's mom nodded and looked at me.

"Well, it's the end of your shift. I'm sorry I wasn't home earlier. I meant to be, but a client called me as I was walking out the door."

"It's fine. It's only ten minutes. I won't put it on my timecard."

"Oh, you should. Please do."

I looked away, feeling like a jerk for even mentioning the overtime. It was only ten minutes. And honestly, I'd forgotten.

I'd been... enjoying myself, I guess.

"I was just bringing down this soup. Then it's time for his meds in about twenty minutes. It's best to take them after eating."

"Thank you so much, Tabby. I'll bring it down."

"Okay."

I stood there, feeling very foolish.

"So, we will see you on Sunday yes? You don't mind working weekends?"

"Not at all. I would work everyday if the service needed me to."

"Alright, well I hope you enjoy your Saturday."

"You too, Ms. Jackson."

I scooped up my things, and stopped.

"Oh and-"

She paused at the top of the stairs.

"Yes?"

"Please say goodnight to Gabriel for me."

"I will. Goodnight Tabitha."

"Goodnight."

I grimaced as soon as I was outside. Why had I said that? He was going to start to think I liked him. Then he'd really turn on the charm. Or worse, he'd feel sorry for me.

Poor delusional Tabitha. The girl who rejected the one guy she liked and missed her chance. The girl who was too afraid to let anyone close.

I sat behind the driver's wheel of my cruddy old car, rubbing my neck. I *did* like him. That was the problem.

This morning I'd wanted to run. Now I wanted to stay. This was work. A job. How crazy was that?

I don't think I'd felt this way since Maryanne's Coffee Shop shut down. That had been my worst paying job by far, but the young owner of the shop had become a friend. Someone who treated me as an equal.

Plus it smelled so good, with all the teas and pastries. It had been warm and inviting, kind of like going home. Except it was much cozier than our home had ever been.

I sighed, realizing I owed her a phone call. And Dennis. And Jackie.

Of course, if I wanted to catch Jackie I had to stay up late. She went out most nights, since hosting fund raising events was her job. And Paris was way ahead of Eastern Time. But on the nights I worked late and came home keyed up, we'd message online or video chat.

I wondered what Jackie would say about the Gabe situation. She had noticed me watching him years before he'd even approached me. She'd teased me about Gabe exactly once. Before she realized how bad I had it.

The girl from the wrong side of the tracks and the jock. Ha ha. But now... well, things were different. We were more than our labels. I guess, we always had been.

Especially Jackie, who everyone had called 'alternative'. Now she was in Paris, dating the owner of an art gallery and wearing the chicest designer clothes on the planet.

I debated about calling her tonight.

I knew what she would say anyway.

She'd probably tell me to go for it. Which was terrible advice. I could not go for it. I needed the job and the money if I ever wanted to get out of this town.

Most of all I needed to protect myself from heartbreak. I had no doubt that's exactly what Gabe Jackson would do. He wouldn't mean to, but a guy like him would move on eventually, even if he was still interested in casually dating me.

I gripped the wheel, forcing myself to focus as I drove home.

I had all day Saturday to get my head on straight. To forget those old dreams of finding someone to love. Someone who didn't see me as a poor, slutty girl from the wrong side of town. Someone strong and sweet like Gabriel.

He was out of my league though. He always had been. A guy like that could have anyone. When he'd wanted me, it had just been because he thought I was easy, just like everyone else at school did. Which was ironic, considering I had been and still was a virgin. No. It was better just to forget all about him and do my job.

And I better.

I had to if I ever wanted a better life for myself.

Even in my small way, I allowed myself a few dreams.

A home of my own. A job I liked. Friends and co-workers who respected me. Who saw me as more than Shabby Tabby, the girl with the porn star body.

It could happen. I knew it. But if I messed up, I'd be stuck waiting tables in this town for the rest of my life.

And I'd never find someone to love.

GABE

I grumbled as I pulled on a sportcoat. I had zero desire to do this. To go out. But my mother had gone to a lot of trouble to arrange it.

And she said that hiding at home was no way to live.

So I was going.

Topher and Lyle were going to be there, as well as a few of mom's friends. Ladies I'd grown up with, who thought of me as a second son. All of that was fine.

I just didn't like where we were going.

Mom just happened to have reserved a party table at the most popular place in town. All the guys went there for pints and gourmet wings on Saturday nights. And after dinner, well, the place was a bar.

A classy bar, but still, it hopped. I knew because I went there every time I was home. But those times I'd been on two feet. This was different. This time I was in a chair.

And everyone who was still around was likely to be there.

The second we got inside my fears were justified.

Pete Chimileci and his entire crew were here. Guys I'd played ball with back in the day. They got up when I came in, making a beeline for us while we waited by the front door.

I reminded myself that I was just as big as them. Just as strong. I was just sitting down.

It wasn't a sign of weakness to be in the chair. It just was what it was. And it wasn't forever.

No one seemed to notice I was self-conscious. They all seemed impressed that I'd gotten injured, calling me a bad-ass and shouting hooyah, even though it wasn't really a combat injury. I got slapped on the back more times than I could count.

Finally, the hostess showed us to our table. I waved as I rolled myself towards the back, grateful for the escape. My mother fussed around, making sure the welcome home centerpiece was perfect and pushing my chair into the place of honor at the head of the table.

"We're early. Perfect."

Yeah, great. I was not happy but I didn't want to upset my mom. Now that I was out, I realized I'd been right to worry. I didn't like it too much, with everyone looking at me. It was one thing to be handicapped at home, but here, there was no getting around it.

Everyone else in the place could walk. And I couldn't.

I wasn't about to feel sorry for myself though. I just didn't like the way people stared. I grit my teeth, determined to do everything in my power to get better.

Even if it meant doing whatever Tabitha told me to do.

Hopefully she'd do a few things *I* wanted too.

A lot of things. Dirty things.

I was staring into space when I saw a gorgeous girl bussing a table. Or rather, I realized I'd been staring at her all along. I knew who she was without her having to turn around.

I sat up straighter. Tabitha worked here? How many fucking jobs did the girl have?

I frowned, realizing she must really be struggling to get the money together to finish school. The thought didn't sit right. Hell, a lot of things I was learning about Tabby didn't sit right.

"She's a lovely girl."

I glanced at my mother. She must have caught me staring. Oops.

"I was surprised you hired her. Did you know who the service was sending over?"

"I did."

I raised my eyebrows. My mother was a stickler for manners and doing the right thing. It seemed weird that she'd hired the sexiest girl in town. Even if I didn't think she'd earned it, Tabby had a reputation.

The girl looked like a porn star. Not that she dressed trampy, but there was no hiding that body. She was a walking boner factory. Everyone said so. I realized it was in the back of my mind too.

Though, that wasn't really fair now, was it?

"Now you listen to me Gabriel Jackson. Just because a person isn't born with money, doesn't mean they are less than. That girl has more grit than most."

I held up my hands.

"Whoa mom, I didn't say anything bad about her."

She made a harrumph sound but she settled down a bit.

"I saw the way you were looking at her, young man. Get your mind out of the gutter. I never believed those rumors about her. And for the record, I've never once seen her with anyone."

I was about to defend myself again when I got stuck on the last thing mom said.

"What do you mean you don't see her with anyone?"

"I mean she doesn't have a lot of friends. Let alone boyfriends."

For some reason, I knew in my gut it was true. Tabby didn't seem like she had fallback. And she didn't read to me like a woman who was getting her needs met either.

Which gave me an opening.

Still, I didn't think my mom was paying attention to which young person dated who.

"Mom. How would you know that?"

"I see things. And I have a very reliable grapevine."

I snorted. But I was still thinking about what she said. I was pretty sure Tabby didn't have a boyfriend. I could just feel it.

Good.

Not that it would have stopped me from trying to steal her away from him. Every second that had ticked by since she walked down those stairs had made me more determined. All was fair in love and war. And I had her at my beck and call until I was on my feet again...

I smiled to myself, suddenly not hating the chair all that much.

"I never said anything bad about her mom. I'm not like that."

She smiled and patted my arm.

"I know you're not. But I'm glad to hear it."

She picked up her menu and I leaned back, deep in thought. Not surprisingly, I was following Tabitha with my eyes as she moved around the bar. I was thinking about the way the guys had talked about her back in high school.

Thats when I saw it.

She was bending over to clear a table near the bar when Pete stuck his hand out and slid it over her ass. I felt rage boil up inside me. If looks could kill, in that moment Pete would have been a pile of ash.

I was halfway to my feet before a searing hot pain tore through my leg. I sat down and grimaced, holding my leg with both hands. *Damn it!* I'd been so angry I'd forgotten.

"Argh-"

I watched as Tabby spun around and said something to him that made Pete turn red and all his friends laugh. Good. I hoped she said he had a small wiener.

Which, I knew from being on the team with him, that he did.

Compared to mine anyway.

My mother was staring at my leg where I still gripped it. I let go and exhaled. The pain was receding. I hadn't made it worse.

"What in the world-"

"It's fine mom. I'll- I'll be right back."

I pushed away from the table and rolled across the room to the bar. Pete was still talking about Tabby, calling her a 'fine piece of ass' and saying how he liked to give it to her 'back in the day'. I knocked my chair right into his legs.

"Hey! Watch it!" He looked surprised to see me. "Jesus Gabe, I thought you were someone else."

"Keep your God damn hands off Tabitha."

"What?"

"Don't touch her again."

He thought I was joking. He nudged his friend in the side. "You can't fault me for wanting to get a squeeze in. Those are some juicy-"

"I mean it Pete. Don't touch her."

He shook his head as a knowing look came into his eyes. "Hey man, if you're fucking her, more power to you."

I just glared at him until the smile faded from his face. I was losing a friend over a girl but I didn't care. The way they were acting was disgusting.

"Jesus man, lighten up. She's a boner factory."

I snarled, even though I had thought the same exact thing twenty minutes ago. I was about to get into a bar fight. I forced myself to cool off a little.

"Let the girl work. She's just doing her job. Show some respect."

"Yeah man, okay."

They were quiet as I rolled away. I didn't go back to the table. I wanted to see her. I had to see if she was okay.

I wheeled myself into the service hall past the bathrooms.

I felt a rush I hadn't felt in a while. Like I was on a mission.

And damn it, I was.

TABBY

"Oh yeah, didn't you hit that back in high school?"

Their words were echoing in my brain as I carried the tray of dirty plates to the back. I could still hearing them laughing. Feel that guy's hand on my body.

No, not a guy. He was a pig.

It was just a reminder that people around here seemed to think I was up for grabs. That they could take what they wanted, when they wanted. I patted the pepper spray in my pocket.

I was safe. It was just a pinch. It wasn't like he'd jumped me in a back alley. Though I had been cornered a few times over the years and narrowly escaped assault. I told myself it wasn't just me. It was any woman who worked around alcohol that had to fend off unwanted advances.

But still, it hurt.

The worst part was how I felt. Vulnerable somehow. He'd taken a chink out of my armor with that move. I felt so exposed out there in the bar. Like I was naked and everyone else was wearing clothes.

I said something unladylike under my breath, taking a moment to try and pull myself together.

This was the last damn thing I needed.

First, Gabe was back. The one guy I'd thought about back in high school was being thrown in my face. Now this. There was a reason I didn't get to go out with a good guy like Gabe.

All the nice guys thought I was a whore.

Oh no, here come the waterworks.

I was about to break my no crying at work rule.

"Tabitha?"

I spun around and there he was. The last person I wanted to see me cry. Gabe was here, at Garrity's. He looked so handsome tonight it took my breath away for a second.

I stared at him, not knowing what to say.

"I didn't know you worked here."

I nodded dumbly, hoping he couldn't see the tears in my eyes. The hallway was dark. Maybe he wouldn't notice.

"Hey, are you alright?"

I blinked, realizing I must look worse than I thought. The thought of Gabe feeling sorry for me was more than I could take. Deep down, I wanted him to like me dammit.

Not pity me.

I exhaled sharply. Now that I'd admitted to myself that my crush was still hanging around, I wanted to squash it immediately. Having feelings for Gabe- even just residual ones from my schoolgirl crush a million years ago- well, it was just asking for trouble.

More than trouble. Pain. I didn't think I could handle more heartbreak. I might crack and not be able to put myself back together again.

Be strong. Stay focused. Keep your distance.

"I'm fine. Can I get you something?"

He was watching me closely.

"I just wanted to say hi."

I nodded, forcing myself to smile. It wasn't a big smile, but I prayed it looked natural. It felt all wrong.

"I think you're in my section. So I'll be coming by in a few minutes."

Dammit. Now he knew I'd seen him come in. In fact, I had been busy trying not to stare at Gabe when the jerks at the bar manhandled me.

Gabe looked so handsome tonight. He'd shaved and put on a dinner jacket and tie. I swallowed, reminding myself that he wasn't interested in me. Not like that. Even if he was being nice.

All he'd ever wanted was sex. He'd been a horny teenager and thought I would be down to screw. Just a roll in the hay in the backseat of his car. That was it. And even that was a million years ago.

I wondered if I'd have the strength to say no if he asked me again.

"TJ you're orders up!"

I jumped at the sound of Sal's voice coming from the kitchen. One of my few friends, the short order cook was an older guy. He had two daughters a few years older than me, part of the reason I think he looked out for me.

He always walked me to my car at the end of the night, which I appreciated.

And he'd just once again saved my ass, because I had been staring at Gabe for three minutes, not saying a damn word.

Idiot.

"I have to get that."

Gabe nodded slowly.

"I'll talk to you tomorrow."

I gave him an odd look. "I'm coming right out to take your order."

He didn't smile.

"I know."

What did he mean he would talk to me tomorrow? The question whirled through my mind as I hustled through my work. I realized he was still watching me as the night wore on.

It was late by the time I got home and I still didn't understand what the hell he meant. One thing was for sure though.

He'd meant something.

I was falling asleep as it hit me. Gabe meant that he wanted to really talk to me. Not like a waitress. Maybe even not like an aid. That's what he meant.

I curled up in my bed, holding my pillow against me.

Why did the thought of talking to Gabe scare the living daylights out of me?

GABE

"Do you want to get some air?"

She nodded.

"Good. We can talk then too."

She stiffened up and I smiled. I didn't care if Tabby wanted to act like nothing had happened last night. Or was happening between *us.* She could try and hide, but I wasn't going to let her.

I was not fooled by the tough act anymore.

Last night, when I'd seen her in that hallway... something had changed. I hated seeing her hurt. And she *was* hurt by those jerks, even though she was good at hiding it.

She was good at hiding everything.

But last night, I had seen her.

For the first damn time, I'd actually seen her.

I'd watched her working her fanny off, doing her job, barely talking to anyone. She didn't stick around or flirt with the customers like most waitresses. She kept her head down, just doing her best.

And yet, she attracted attention anyway.

Every man in the place had his eyes on her. I could tell what most of them were thinking too. I cringed, wondering what it must be like to get hit on by everyone, all the time.

I always thought women liked attention from guys. But what Tabitha went through on a daily basis... just because of the way she looked... well, it fucking pissed me off.

Especially after one of those cretins had laid hands on her.

I wondered how many times that had happened to her. Probably more times than she could count. I started to understand why she'd turned me down on the beach all those years ago.

She'd thought I was one of them. Just out to score. To get a chance to brag to my friends that I'd had a piece of her.

Well, I wasn't like them and I would prove it to her. Yeah, I wanted to touch her. So bad it hurt. But I wanted to protect her too.

And when I touched her, she wouldn't have that hunted look in her eyes. No, I'd take my time. I'd wait until she was sweet and soft and willing in my arms.

I grit my teeth and wheeled myself out the back.

"Don't you want a jacket?"

I shook my head, and grabbed the scarf and hat she tossed at me. I grinned as she tugged on her jacket. She looked so cute today, with her soft curls and button nose. I could tell she was trying to downplay her curves with yet another oversized shirt, but it wasn't working.

I'd like to see her in something pretty. Feminine. Something soft that I could rub up against. I grinned at her and winked.

"I give off heat like a furnace, babe."

She gave me a look as she shut the door behind me, following me down the path to the sidewalk. She caught the handles to the chair and held on. I was about to protest when I realized I could smell her when she was this close. I took a deep breath. She smelled like cookies.

"You don't have to do that."

She clucked her tongue.

"Just on hills. The breaks on these chairs are notoriously bad."

I twisted my neck to look up at her. She looked good from this angle. Hell, the woman looked good from all angles. I couldn't wait to try a few of them out.

"No shit?"

She nodded.

"Yeah, it's bad. Once you are rolling you can really pick up speed. Promise me you'll be careful."

She frowned at me, utterly serious. She looked worried. I felt a warm flush spread through me.

Tabby was worried about *me.*

She *did* like me. I knew I wasn't imagining it.

"I will."

We didn't talk the rest of the way to the water. It was only a few blocks but in the chair, it felt much longer. A few of our neighbors waved and I realized I didn't feel self-conscious about the chair for the first time.

How could I with this gorgeous woman with me?

I pictured us taking the same walk, but hand in hand. I would pull her into my arms and steal a kiss whenever I wanted to. She'd sigh and smile and curl into my chest.

Then we'd go home and cook together. Or shower. And make the bed bounce.

Hell, I had a feeling we would break the bed.

I decided I'd buy extra mattresses if that was what it took. That would be a small price to pay for having Tabby in my life.

I just had to get her on board with sticking around once I was out of the chair.

She pushed me down to the bottom of the hill and up the slight incline to the edge of the parking lot. The sand started there, so I was stuck in the parking lot. But the air was clean and salty and there was a low fence for Tabitha to perch that juicy butt of hers on.

"Take a load off Tabby."

She shrugged and sat on the edge of the wooden fence. She stared out at the water. I stared at her.

It was... nice.

Finally I took a deep breath and dove in.

"They won't bother you again."

"What?"

"Those idiots last night at Garrity's."

She was looking at me now, not the waves. The look on her face was heartbreaking. She was surprised enough to let her guard down and I could see it all- every bit of pain those jerks had caused her.

Then she looked away and the shutters closed again.

"I don't need your help."

I stared at her. She did need me dammit. She was just going to have to come to terms with it.

"Tabby... don't be like that."

She refused to look at me, crossing her arms over her chest.

"Why bother? Both of us will be out of this stupid town soon enough. It's better not to make waves."

"I wanted to beat the hell out of them."

She looked at me with her eyebrows raised. I could tell she didn't believe me.

"I thought those guys were your buddies. You were always eating with them at school."

I grinned at her. I felt like the sun had just come out.

"You noticed who I ate lunch with?"

She blushed furiously and stood up.

"We should go back."

I caught her hand and squeezed it.

"I noticed where you sat too."

"Gabe- don't."

Her voice was soft and pleading. If I hadn't been in the damn chair I would have kissed her then and there. As it was, I was going to need to spell it out for her.

"Come here."

Her eyes were wide as I tugged her closer.

"What?"

"You know what."

She was being difficult. To hell with it. I yanked her hand and she stumbled into me, landing on my lap. I held her firmly as she tried to extricate herself.

If I didn't know she liked me, I wouldn't have done it. I didn't want to harass the girl. But I knew she felt the same way. She wanted me back.

And I was tired of waiting.

So I lied.

"Gabe!"

"Don't move- you're hurting me!"

She froze immediately, her eyes searching my face.

"Are you alright?"

I smiled at her stupidly, overwhelmed by the feeling of her in my arms. She was so petite. And soft. And squishy.

In a ridiculously delicious way.

"No."

"If you aren't alright, why are you smiling?"

I just smiled at her some more.

"This is nice."

"What is nice? I'm crushing you!"

I nodded.

"That's the nice part."

She rolled her eyes.

"Okay Gabe, this is silly. I'm your nurse, remember?"

I rested my chin on her shoulder.

"Do you really want to get up?"

She hesitated and I had my answer.

I let my hands slide up her back to her face and turned her head just so. Then I swooped in, kissing her hard. She let out a startled squeak but didn't move.

After a second, she started kissing me back.

Hmmm... delicious. Tabitha's lips were soft, her breath sweet. Her skin felt like silk under my hands. I tasted her with my tongue, just a little bit and was rewarded when she sighed again.

I was breathing heavily when we stopped a few minutes later.

She looked startled and confused. I smiled at her.

"I've been wanting to do that since the eighth grade."

"You have?"

"You know I have."

She blinked and I kissed her again. This time she didn't relax. She was stiff in my arms. I leaned back to look at her and she jumped up like a jack in the box. I reached for her hand but she wouldn't look at me.

"Hey, don't go."

"We need to- get back. It's almost time for your meds and-"

"I don't want any pain meds."

She glanced at me, pushing her hair back where I'd messed it up. She looked fucking gorgeous standing there with her cheeks pink and her lips bruised from my kisses.

"You know, kissing releases endorphins. Nature's pain medicine."

She shot me a startled look. She probably thought I was a dumb jock. But I'd been looking things up online all week.

Especially things that might be good arguments for getting her into bed with me.

Endorphins, man. Got to love them.

"See? You healed me."

She rolled her eyes but she was smiling.

"Come on, let's go."

I was grinning as I rolled myself back up the hill to my mom's house. Tabby held on the whole time, but I used my arms too. I needed the work out.

I was feeling pent up, and the day had just started.

I pulled my scarf into my lap to cover the bulge there. It didn't work. I shrugged. My cock was just too big.

I was surprised she hadn't said something when she was on my lap. I'd done my best not to poke her with the beast, but it was kind of hard to ignore.

I was known for my massive unit. And at the moment it was hard as a damn rocket. In fact, the guys in basic had called me Torpedo after seeing me in the showers. The nickname had stuck with me as I climbed the ranks, though I tried to discourage it.

Tabby ran off to get my lunch and pills ready and I was able to cover my hard on with a blanket. I was wondering if she would massage me again. I hoped so, even if it was excruciating.

Maybe if I was lucky, she'd let me give *her* a massage.

I closed my eyes and let myself imagine that.

Gabe was dozing on the couch when I came down with his tray. I chewed my lip, not sure if I should wake him. I would love it if he slept all damn day and stopped trying to charm me.

Despite my best efforts, it was working.

I'd even let him kiss me. I had no idea what had come over me. It was irresponsible to say the least. And bad, bad, bad.

Stupid and dangerous and *bad.*

I sighed. He needed his meds. I nudged his shoulder lightly.

"Are you asleep?"

He shook his head and cracked an eye at me.

"Just daydreaming."

"About what?"

He grinned at me and I had a sudden urge to disappear. I knew what that smile said. It said he'd been daydreaming about *me.* And it made me feel all warm and goosebumpy all over.

I shook my head, trying to be cool.

"Why did I ask?"

"It's obvious."

"Oh, it is, is it?"

"You're curious about the inner thoughts of such a strong, manly... man."

I laughed. I couldn't help it. He was so funny. And he was flirting with me.

I wasn't used to this kind of flirting. Usually guys just commented on the way I looked. But this was different. Sweeter. I didn't know what to make of it.

That was a lie. I liked it. I liked it a lot.

For the first time in my life, a man was flirting with me. The right way. No grabbing or suggestive comments. Just... making me feel appreciated.

Making me laugh.

Either way though, I didn't have time for an entanglement. I had to work. And this *was* a job, no matter how ridiculously charming he was being.

He sat up and patted the couch beside him.

"Sit with me."

"No, Gabe."

"Why not?"

"You can't kiss me again."

"Why not?"

I sighed heavily. He was being way too persistent. He reminded me of a child. Oddly enough I found it endearing.

Annoying, but endearing.

And really only annoying because I was having trouble ignoring him.

I put on my best nurse voice. Also known as my Sunday school voice. Though I'd never taught Sunday school.

"I'm working."

He smiled.

"Oh that. Well, what are you doing later?"

"Working."

"Are you waiting tables tonight?"

I sighed.

"No. Today I work until five."

"So, I will start kissing you at 5:03."

I laughed again. But I shook my head.

"Gabe, be serious. You're cute but don't bother."

He perked up like a puppy hearing a can opener.

"I'm cute?"

"No! I mean, I just meant- oh, never mind."

He batted his eyelashes at me. I had to get out of here. If I stayed around him I was going to cave. As much as I needed the money, I needed to not get my soul crushed more.

And I had a feeling that Gabe could crush me. Without even trying.

My eyes watered suddenly.

Oh no. Please, please, please do not start weeping here.

For someone who never cried, I was turning into a damn sprinkler.

"You should eat. You were supposed to take your meds five minutes ago."

He smiled at me, raising his eyebrows.

"You are so strict. I can handle that though."

I bit my lip to stop myself from asking him what he meant. I shouldn't have worried though. He picked up his sandwich and took a bite. Then he kept talking.

"The military trained me to withstand all sorts of adverse conditions."

"Is that so?"

He ate one of the celery spears I'd cut up and put on the plate instead of chips. I was going to get him healthy. He seemed to like the food I made him, thankfully.

Oh, but he wasn't done yet.

“Freezing temperatures. Sleet. Snow. Rain. Hunger. Hard-hearted women."

My mouth opened. His words were light but he was staring at me with a serious look in his eyes. Like he could see right through me.

"So go ahead. Dish it out woman. I was born to suffer."

That sounded like... a promise.

"Hell, if it's you doing the torturing, I might even enjoy it."

I stood there, frozen to the spot. I was a deer in headlights in front of his high beams. Just waiting for him to make me another trophy.

I shook myself mentally. Reminded myself that I was no one's trophy. I was a person, not a challenge. Even though I was enjoying his attention, it would not end well for me if I gave in.

When I gave in, unless I put some space between the two of us.

"Here are your meds. Then I think you should lie down for a nap."

He took his pills obediently.

"Will you rub my back again?"

I inhaled at the suggestive look in his eyes. Suggestive, but not crude. It made me feel... warm inside.

"Not today."

He grinned at me.

"Can I rub *you*?"

I stood up straight and stepped back.

"That's not funny, Gabe."

"I'm not joking. You work so hard, I thought you could use it."

I stared at him, my mouth open like a fish. How was I supposed to answer that? I probably did need a back rub. To be honest, I didn't think I'd ever had one. I wondered what it would be like, having someone put their energy and care into you. Taking the time to really make me feel nice.

I didn't know. And now was not the time to find out.

I left him alone to finish his sandwich. One thing I knew for sure, I had to keep my wits about me. This was a dangerous situation, not to mention unprofessional.

I wanted to be a nurse, dammit. It was an important job. It meant something.

And that meant keeping my distance from my way too adorable patient.

GABE

I groaned with effort as I took another step. My arms were straining from holding myself up on the bars. I put a tiny bit of weight on my injured leg with each step. It was harder than it looked, walking without really walking.

My other leg was even getting tired from doing most of the work.

I had been eager to start physical therapy. I'd thought it would be a cakewalk for a tough guy like me.

I was wrong.

I felt like I was back in basic, eating dirt with my SO's foot on my back while I did pushups.

"Take a quick breather."

My physical therapist Danny was on the other side of the rail, guiding me along. I bent my leg, leaning on the bars. I realized I was sweating, like I'd just lifted or gone for a run. That was a good reminder of why I was here.

To walk again. To run. To be able to lift a woman up in my arms.

Not just any woman either.

One in particular.

"Your girlfriend is here."

I looked up, my eyes seeking her out immediately. It was weird but Tabby looked different in here. Nervous. Like she didn't think she belonged.

I still drank her up like a cold glass of water on a hot day.

She'd been avoiding me all week. Which was challenging considering she'd been at my house for eight hours a day. But somehow she managed it.

First, there was the cleaning. She'd spent hours with her non-toxic sprays and polishes. She'd even vacuumed. Twice.

The woman had cleaned the whole damn house instead of sitting and talking to me.

Then, there were the books.

Nursing books. Paperbacks. Magazines.

The girl would bring me my food and pills, ask me how I was feeling and then sit her fine ass down as far away as possible to bury her head in a book. And she'd stay that way until her timer went off and it was time to tend to me again.

I felt like a Goddamn houseplant.

I didn't like it.

I didn't fucking like it at all.

Tabitha was shutting me out completely. And she was doing a damn good job of it. I tried not to be mad. I knew *why* she was doing it. She was afraid I would kiss her again. Not because she didn't like it.

Because she did.

She liked me and she was too chickenshit to admit it.

And that *did* make me mad.

She set her bag down on a chair by the door and shrugged out of her coat. I noticed how adorable she looked in her oversized black top. This one was more of a sweater than her usual button down, and it clung to her chest. She tugged it away from her body but static cling brought it right back.

I said a small hallelujah for static cling as I let my eyes wander over her body.

That long top of hers even hugged her tiny waist and round ass. As usual, her long curvy legs were encased in those worn-in jeans. Her cheeks were a dusky pink from the cold air outside. I stared at her hungrily, wanting to toss her over my shoulder and carry her to the closest bed.

She probably thought the loose top made her blend in, or hid her curves.

She was wrong.

I could see more of her than I ever had before. And I liked it. My cock did too.

He made his feelings known with a distinct twitch.

"You're late."

She flinched, looking like a beat dog. I hated that. I wanted her to roll her eyes at me and give me some sass. I was starting to realize that there were three Tabby's: the tough one, the weary one, and the real one. Today, she was too weary to be tough and too scared to be real.

I wanted the real one, dammit. The Tabby who melted into my arms when I'd kissed her at the beach. The one who noticed who I sat with and cared what I ate.

"My car broke down."

I took another step. If I could walk, I could get a job. Get my own place.

Get the girl.

"Is it okay?"

She bit her lip, her eyes on my feet.

"Your car. Is it okay?"

"Not really."

"How did you get here then?"

"The bus. Excuse me a minute."

She hurried away, obviously not in the mood to talk. I frowned. The recovery center was almost an hour away in a car. If she'd taken the bus it would have taken two hours, even with her being late.

So, she'd known her car was broken down this morning and still not called me to ask for a ride. That was just stupid. I knew it was her pride, as usual.

Her Goddamn pride was ruining everything.

I grunted as I turned around to go back the other way.

"Had enough?"

"No."

Danny let out a low whistle.

"Damn, dude. Your girlfriend's hot."

I gave Danny a look.

"She's not my girlfriend. She's my aid."

He shook his head.

"That's too bad, man. She's mega fine."

I agreed with him, but I didn't want to talk about her like a piece of meat.

"So if she's not your girlfriend does that mean I can ask her out?"

"No."

He chuckled at my vehemence.

"Ah- I knew it. You do like her! I don't blame you man."

"Just leave her alone, she's working."

I took another step, realizing I'd made the return trip in half the time. I collapsed into the chair with Danny's help. My legs were fucking shaking like jello.

"You did good, man. You were really motoring on the way back."

I nodded. He didn't realize how much he'd pissed me off. I understood why Tabby tried to cover herself up. It must suck to have every guy commenting on her looks, or worse.

I cringed to think about how Pete had touched her while she was working. I wondered how often that kind of stuff went down.

That's why she was being so damn skittish with me. Why she was fighting this thing between us. Because of all the other idiots in the world who couldn't see past her looks.

I wasn't sure which made things worse; her insanely sexy body or her model beautiful face. It was all distracting to guys, who never stopped to think that she was a person with feelings, not just an object of lust.

Tabby came back in and I felt the air change. She did that, just by walking into the room. Everything was brighter. Everything was better.

"Okay, I'm supposed to show you his daily exercises and how to rub him down after."

She nodded and crossed her arms, not coming any closer. Danny was too stupid to notice her defensive posture. Arms protectively over her chest, her stunning eyes wary. Something twisted inside me and cracked open.

I wanted to hold her. Protect her. Love her until she opened up like a flower.

But I couldn't. Not until I was out of this damn chair.

And the world kept turning...

I forced myself to focus as Danny wheeled me over to the exercise bench. I clenched my jaw. I could do this.

"I'm Danny."

"Tabitha."

"Great, let's get started."

"Okay, so you start at the knee. The magnesium oil goes on first, then the castor oil. The vitamin E is good for healing. After you rub it in you can wrap a heating pad over it. Use a hand towel or an old t-shirt under it. See?"

I watched as the physical therapist moved his fingers on Gabe's bare leg. His thigh was still muscular, with creamy skin that was edged in pink ridges where his wound had been. I ignored the fluttery feelings I got from looking at his naked flesh and focused.

I could see that the scar tissue was getting thicker. That was good. He was getting better.

Now he just had to strengthen the muscles without jarring the tendons or ligaments. He could walk again, though he'd probably need a cane. At least, I hoped he would.

"Here are some diagrams with the exercises in case you need reminders."

I took them numbly, feeling like a jerk. It felt wrong to pretend I was sticking around. I wasn't going to be the one helping Gabe with any of this. He needed me and I was about to bail on him.

I was a coward. I knew it. But I was also a pragmatist.

And I needed to protect myself from him.

From all of this.

"Okay, that's it. Good job, man."

"Thanks Danny."

The therapist smiled at me.

"I'll see you both next week."

I grabbed my coat and bag, not bothering to correct him. Hopefully by next week they'd have a new aid. Maybe a real nurse.

Not a dropout like me.

"Where are you going?"

I stared at Gabe.

"To catch the bus."

"Don't be ridiculous. I drove here."

I shifted my bag on my shoulder. I didn't want to be in a long car ride with Gabe. It would be impossible to avoid him.

"I thought your mom was here."

He grinned.

"I can drive. It's my left leg that's messed up, remember? I just need help getting the chair in and out."

I bit my lip. He was being friendly. He hadn't seemed all that happy to see me when I walked in late.

"Come on, Tabby. I'm not taking no for an answer."

I followed him down the hallway to the elevator. We rode down in silence. I had to be at Garrity's in an hour and a half. I really didn't have time to catch the bus.

I sighed and helped him put the chair in the back of the car.

"How did you manage when you got here?"

"Danny knew to come out and get me set up."

"Your mom is really amazing."

I meant that. She was a really cool lady. She'd always been nice to me. And she was taking amazing care of Gabe.

Of course, it wasn't just his mother. Any woman alive would bend over backwards to help him. He was so charming and handsome and manly and...

Shut up Tabby.

I stared straight ahead while Gabe tried to make small talk. I gave him one word answers and checked my phone. I didn't want to be rude, but I did want to discourage him.

Plus, I knew he would be annoyed when I told him what I'd done. Not just annoyed. Pissed off. Being a coward, I waited until he pulled into town and drove right to my street.

Which was pretty weird considering I'd never told him where I lived.

"Sorry if Danny was overly friendly."

I gave him a startled look. I hadn't realized he'd noticed. The PT guy had been flirting with me the whole time.

"I'll tell him to chill for next week."

"Don't bother." I bit my lip. "You are just going to have to teach someone else anyway."

Gabe gave me a sharp look. The SUV wasn't small, but suddenly I felt like there was no air in the space. He was a big guy and he felt close.

Too close.

"What?"

I exhaled, hoping he wouldn't freak.

"I put in my notice."

His eyes got wide and he cursed.

"Why Tabby?"

I looked away, not answering him. He grabbed my shoulders and turned me towards him. His eyes searched my face.

"Because I kissed you? That's fucking bullshit."

I pulled back and shook my head.

"I don't have time for this- for any of this."

His eyes narrowed and he reached for me again, taking my hands.

"Don't. I have to go... I have to go to work. I'm going to pick up some extra shifts."

He stared at me, a muscle ticking in his jaw. He didn't let go of my hands though. He squeezed them. Hard.

"You'd rather sling drinks and wings for guys who would treat you like a piece of meat?"

My mouth opened but no words came out.

"I wouldn't do that to you, Tabby. I fucking respect you."

He looked furious. I didn't know what to say. I shook my head as if to clear it. I realized he was squeezing my hands so hard the fingertips were turning white.

"I'll stay on until they find someone new. It's not like I was going to be here much longer anyway."

He didn't say anything for a long minute. Eventually he let go of my hands. I opened the door and gave him one last look.

"Gabe..."

His head jerked towards me. He looked like he was in pain. I felt my stomach twist at the look in his eyes.

"I'm sorry."

GABE

I finished my dinner, staring glumly into space. My mom had made one of my childhood favorites tonight. Sweet potato casserole. It had been years since I'd had it. I'm sure it was delicious.

I couldn't taste a damn thing.

I thanked her as she cleaned up. I'm pretty sure she noticed how moody I was but she didn't say anything. It was a good thing too. I didn't know how to explain that I was upset because I couldn't get a woman.

Not just any woman. A girl who had tantalized me since puberty. A girl who wanted me back, but kept hovering out of reach.

A girl who needed me as much as I needed her. And I wasn't just talking sex, though I wanted to have lots and lots of sex with her. I had a feeling we both needed something *more* out of life.

Something real.

Something we might be able to build together.

Only Tabby was running away from it. From me. And since I was in this damn chair, I couldn't exactly chase her down.

I was still sitting at the table downstairs a half an hour later. The sun was setting through the sliding glass doors. I could see it glinting off the waves in the distance. It was another beautiful night of me doing absolutely fucking nothing.

Fuck this.

It was time to take the bull by the horns. I pulled out my phone and texted Tabitha. Within a few moments she had texted me back. I wondered if she was as lonely as I was.

If she wanted to see me as bad as I wanted to see her.

Don't do this. Don't quit

IT HAD nothing to do with you

I want to talk

I'm working Gabe

Fine. I'll come to you.

NOTHING. Radio silence. Not a peep.

Fine, if she wanted to be like this, I was going to have to play dirty. Or at least be more aggressive about getting what I wanted.

I was tired of waiting for her to come around.

"Mom?"

Her head popped down the stairwell a minute later. I knew she'd been sitting up there worrying about me. I ignored the pinprick of guilt I felt. I would gladly cheer up and make my mom happy.

As soon as I got what I wanted.

Tabby.

"Can you drop me in town? I'll get a cab back."

"Do you want to drive? You can use my car."

"No. I'm going to have a drink."

She lit up. "Oh, are you meeting the guys?" I nodded, thinking it wasn't quite a lie. Hell, they were probably all there anyway, bellied up to the bar.

"Give me five, okay?"

She nodded and disappeared to give me some privacy. I rolled into the bathroom and hoisted myself up to stare at the mirror. I had a faint shadow but didn't want to take the time to shave. I splashed my face, brushed my teeth and combed my hair. All while standing on one leg.

Doesn't matter, Gabe. Doesn't make you less of a man.

I smirked suddenly.

It didn't mean I couldn't please one cranky Tabby cat. My dick still worked. So did my fingers. And my tongue.

I would make her squeal I decided. I'd make her beg.

I didn't care how many lovers she'd had. I would be the one to impress her. To break down her walls and get at the gooey center.

I would be the best.

I rubbed some deodorant under my arms and changed my shirt. I even stuck a couple condoms in my wallet. Maybe she'd invite me back to her place.

Maybe I'd insist that we go there to talk. Then I'd work my magic on her.

Hell yeah, this was going down.

I was going to get my woman.

"You ready?"

I nodded to my mom and wheeled myself out the back.

"I'm ready."

TABBY

I counted my tips. Fifty bucks so far. Dammit. It was a slow night for everyone, blustery cold outside. But I couldn't afford slow nights.

I needed every penny to afford a new place and another crack at school. I had to get out of this damn town before I turned into what they thought I was.

A tramp.

Because I was inches away from giving in to Gabe.

Then what would I be? The girl from the wrong side of the tracks who tumbled into bed with the star quarterback. The war hero who would move on to greener pastures as soon as he was healed. All he'd have to do was snap his fingers at this point. I was that close.

And I would be stuck here, with nothing. Fair game for all the other jerks. The ones who didn't make my heart race or my stomach flutter.

I stuffed the money in my apron and froze.

Dark green eyes were staring at me from across the bar. Piercing eyes that went straight through me. My heart started to pound.

Gabe was here. He was sitting by himself at the end of the bar. I frowned. How the hell did he get up into that chair? He could have hurt himself!

I was across the bar before I thought about what people might think.

Gabe wasn't even trying to hide that he was watching me. He had a dark look on his face and a pint in his hand.

"What are you doing here?"

He took a sip of his beer.

"It's a bar. I'm drinking."

I took a step back. He was acting weird. Like he didn't like me. Not even a little.

Maybe he didn't.

I had told him I was leaving.

"How did you get into the stool- you shouldn't have done that."

"Why not?"

"You could have hurt yourself- your leg-"

He smirked at me suggestively.

"It's just one leg Tabby. The rest of my body works just fine. Believe me."

I took another step back, feeling uncertain. I realized people were staring at us. We were bordering on making a scene. I shook my head and went back to work.

I tried not to look over at him. He was surrounded by the local guys almost immediately. I noticed that everyone was trying to impress him. It was just like high school.

He was in the center of it all. Just like usual.

And I was on the outskirts.

I kept my head down, stealing a glance at him now and then. He looked so handsome it made my insides twist. And I thought I caught him looking at me a few times.

Was he here to see me? Like he'd said in his text?

If he was here to see me, then why was he ignoring me?

I went into the stockroom as it got late to start setting up for the morning shift. I bent over to grab a stack of napkins. That's when I heard it.

The heavy metal door creaked and slammed shut behind me.

Gabe sat there in his chair. He didn't say anything. He just watched me. He reached up and locked the door behind him.

Then he smiled. It was not a nice smile. It was a dangerous smile.

"What are you doing?"

"I told you. I wanted to talk."

"Not now, Gabe. I'm working."

He crossed his arms.

"It's not busy. All the other waitresses are sitting on their asses at the bar counting tips. But not you."

I raised my chin. If he was angry at me- if he wanted a confrontation- I had to be ready for it.

I had to be strong.

"No, not me."

He laughed. It sounded bitter. I wondered if he'd had too much to drink.

"You work harder than anyone I know. Not just at the job. At keeping people away."

I blinked.

"Your drunk."

He wheeled closer and I backed up until my shoulders were against the metal shelves that were bolted to the wall. He reached out and traced his finger along the top of my apron. I shivered from the feeling of his hand through my clothes.

"Just a little buzzed."

My eyes got wide as he reached for me. No- not for me. He reached *past* me.

He grunted as he used the metal bars to hoist himself to his feet. I was afraid to move. Afraid I would hurt him.

Afraid of what was about to happen.

He stood over me, inches away. He was so big... I'd forgotten how tall he was. How wide his shoulders were. He dwarfed me. I couldn't see anything but him.

"You're not quitting."

I lifted my chin and stared him right in the eye. It was hard, but I made myself do it.

"I am."

"I won't let you." His lips quirked. "I need you."

My heart did a little flip flop. I looked to the side, trying to ignore how his closeness was affecting me. I felt hot and cold and-

His fingertips brushed my cheek.

"Tabitha..."

Then he was gripping my face, turning me to face him. I realized what he was doing right before his lips caught mine. He kissed me firmly. He moaned as he tasted me, like I tasted delicious. I let out a little whimper as he leaned closer, his chest brushing mine.

Then everything changed. He growled and pulled me against him with one arm. I was wrapped in his strength as he forced my lips apart. His tongue was in my mouth, taking what he wanted. There was no teasing this time. No playfulness.

Just raw, primal hunger.

And so help me God, I kissed him right back.

Gabe kept on touching me, stroking my back and sides. I leaned into his touch like a cat. Wanting more- wanting- I didn't even know what it was I wanted.

But Gabe did.

His hand slid lower and I let him guide my leg up so that he could get even closer. I felt his hardness against me and gasped. He was huge and he was burning hot. Even through his jeans.

It woke me out of the stupor I was in.

I shook my head wildly.

"No! Gabe- stop!"

He stopped and stared down at me, his jaw ticking. He looked so different from the charming, sweet man I knew during daylight hours. This man looked desperate. Angry.

Starving.

"Please stop."

He swallowed and stepped back slightly.

I felt the cold air rush between us. Like we'd created a vacuum where our bodies had pressed together. There had been heat and touch and now there was nothing.

"Tabby... why won't you let me in?"

I couldn't look at him.

"In what? My pants?"

"That's not what I meant." He smirked. "But yeah, I want that too."

"I'm not a tramp. I'm not what- everyone says."

He gripped my chin and made me look at him. I didn't want to. I was so afraid of what I'd see.

His eyes were burning. Fierce.

"I know."

I exhaled in a whoosh. He meant it. He wasn't just trying to get off with the town slut. At least I thought that's what I saw in his eyes.

Bang bang bang!

"TJ! You in there? We're closing up."

"Be right out!"

I looked at Gabe. He hadn't moved.

"Gabe, I need to go."

He cursed.

"Fine. But we are continuing this conversation."

"What's the point?"

He growled and yanked me against him. He kissed me hard, his body unyielding, his tongue pushing into my mouth. I realized my feet were dangling off the floor. Even injured, the man could lift me without breaking a sweat.

He set me down and looked at me.

"That's the point."

Then he lowered himself into his chair and wheeled away.

GABE

I waited by the door, refusing to leave with Topher and Lyle. Tabby shook her head when the line cook asked if he needed to get rid of me like the last guy.

Apparently, this sort of thing had happened before.

It should have upset me that other guys had been with her, but instead it made me more resolved. I was not putting up with this any longer. She was not going to lie to herself, or to me.

She was not going to run away.

If she could look me in the eye, and tell me she didn't want me as much as the other guys she'd been with, fine. But I knew she couldn't. She was a lot of things, but she wasn't a liar. I was betting on it.

I waited as she pulled on her coat and waved to her last few co-workers as they shut the lights down. She held her folded apron in her hand and stared at me. Without a word we went outside.

It was starting to snow.

"Should I get a cab?"

"I got my car back. It's... not very nice though."

"I don't care."

She sighed and led me down the block to her car. It was, as she said, not very nice. I noticed that she'd parked under a bright streetlight.

Good girl.

She was smart to look out for herself like that. But from now on she didn't have to. I was going to do it for her.

"Gabe... what are we doing?"

Standing there in the soft glow of the streetlight, with the snow falling around her, she looked like an angel. I stared at her hungrily, my eyes roving over her perfect face. Her beautiful eyes were worried.

Worried, but also hopeful.

"I'm not going to hurt you."

She waited but I didn't say anything else. I wasn't going to spell it out for her. That would come later, when we were in her bed. Then I would tell her that she was going to be mine from this point forward.

That I was keeping her.

She swallowed and looked away. Then she nodded and unlocked the car and I knew I had won. I used my arms to heave myself into the old vinyl seat. Tabby folded my chair and put it in the back.

I couldn't help but notice that the beat-up old car was neat as a pin. I smiled. She was conscientious. There was no arguing that.

Tabby's hands were white when she rested them on the steering wheel.

"We should go to your place."

"I'd rather not." I grunted. I wanted to get to her place. I wanted to get to know her dammit. Plus, I assumed it was more private. "Why?"

"Mine isn't wheelchair friendly."

I grit my teeth. She was still keeping me out. Holding me at arm's length. But so be it.

She was coming with me at least. She wasn't fighting me anymore. I nodded, deciding to take what I could get.

"Fine."

She pulled out into traffic, driving carefully in the snow. I was tempted to tell her to stop at the beach. It was so romantic in the snow.

But there wasn't much room in the car for getting horizontal. Besides, I wanted our first time together to be in a bed.

And once I started kissing her, I knew I wasn't going to be able to stop.

On a bed, it was an even playing field. I could move freely, as long as I didn't put too much weight on my injured leg. I could make her mine without feeling like a cripple.

I looked out the window and smiled. It was happening. Tonight.

Tonight, Tabby was going to be mine.

TABBY

I glanced at my phone. It was late, but I'd missed a call from Maryanne and Jackie. Jacks had even texted me, asking me about Gabe. I shoved the phone back into my purse and looked at Gabe.

"Did you take your pills already?"

He just looked at me. He was on the couch, waiting for me to sit down. I perched on the edge of it instead, my jacket still on. I was pretty much ready to run out of there at a moment's notice.

"You're off duty. Come."

He patted the seat next to him and I chewed my lip, considering. After a minute, I realized I looked like an idiot and sat. Gabe reached for my chest and I flinched back. Gabe gave me an odd look. I realized he had been reaching for the zipper of my jacket.

I held perfectly still as he pulled the zipper down and exposed my tight work t-shirt. He leaned back again and quirked a smile at me.

"Aren't you going to take it off?"

I nodded jerkily, feeling like a freak. I was so damn nervous. It's not like I didn't want this. Want him... I did. I just, well, I'd never done it before.

Maybe you should tell him that, dummie.

I tried to imagine telling Gabe I was a virgin at twenty-two. He'd probably laugh himself silly. Or think I was lying. I wasn't sure which was worse.

So, I said nothing.

I shrugged the jacket off and left it behind me, feeling awkward. He gave me a friendly smile, lulling me into a sense of calm. Then he reached out lightning quick and grabbed me.

Before I knew it I was sitting in his lap.

"Gabe!"

He grinned, his hands holding my hips firmly in place.

"What?"

"I thought you wanted to- to talk!"

He was looking at me like I was something good to eat. And he was starving. He shook his head.

"Later."

Then he was kissing me. I worried that I was putting weight on his leg and tried to move but he wouldn't let me budge an inch. I pulled in a shaky breath as his tongue slid into my mouth and tangled with mine.

It felt nice.

It felt more than nice.

It felt amazing.

Before I knew it, I was kissing him back, sighing with pleasure as he pressed our bodies together.

I felt his hands start to move over my clothes, molding and cupping each curve. He moaned loudly as his hand closed over my breast for the first time.

"Jesus Tabby..."

He twisted smoothly until somehow I was lying beneath him. He made a sexy, deep sound as he settled between my thighs. He kissed me again and after a minute I forgot that this was the first time.

The first time I'd let anyone touch me, or get this close.

It felt natural and right and so, so good I could hardly believe it. He seemed to think so too. Gabe told me I was beautiful in between kissing me. He told me he wanted me.

He told me how bad.

But then he reached for my top. I froze, cringing when he started to unbutton my shirt.

"Wait-"

"What's wrong?"

He was staring at me, breathing hard. How the hell was I supposed to tell him I felt self-conscious about my breasts? They were too big and heavy and just- out there.

I usually wore two bras when I worked. In fact, I was wearing two right now.

I didn't want him to think I was a freak.

"Tell me, Tabitha."

"Please. Don't make me say it out loud. I'm a freak, okay?"

He just stared at me.

"You are not a freak. You're freakin' *beautiful.*"

I exhaled and closed my eyes. He thought that now, but what would he think when my clothes came off?

"Can't you just... turn the lights off or something?"

And he shook his head slowly.

"No."

I opened my mouth but no words came out.

"Let me see you."

"I'm... not normal."

He laughed and rested his forehead on mine.

"No, you are not normal. You're better than normal."

He kissed me softly, his fingers sliding over my shirt.

"Much, much better."

I closed my eyes and prayed for strength. If I was going to be with him- even if it was just this once- I was going to have to let him undress me.

I let go of his hand and leaned back on the couch.

"Okay."

GABE

D*ear God in Heaven.*

I stared down at the gorgeous girl beneath me. Her eyes were heavy lidded as she stared up at me. Her lips were pink and juicy. Her cheeks were flushed.

And her tits- her glorious tits were almost exposed.

Just one- more- button-

I moaned at the sight of them. Her plain black bra held them down, creating two delicious round mounds above. The bra was big, but she was still spilling out of it.

Yes, Tabby was blessed in the breast department. And then some.

I leaned down to kiss the juicy tops and moaned at the silky softness under my lips.

"Hmmm... perfect..."

Even perfect was an understatement. Her tits were phenomenal. Better than perfect.

The girl deserved a Goddamn blue ribbon for them. An award. A plaque to hang on the wall that said:

'Tabby Peterson.The best tits ever.'

I reached behind her narrow back to unclasp her bra, while nibbling on her ear. I tugged her shirt off her shoulders. She made a squeaky sound of alarm, like a cute little kitty.

"What if your mom comes down here?"

I lifted my head.

"Do you want to go into the bedroom?"

"Yes. Please."

She nodded shyly and looked up at me. I felt my cock lurch in my jeans. This was happening. It was finally *finally* happening.

I was getting my hands on Tabitha.

Her and her sinful, ridiculous, mind bending curves.

I just had to get both of us into the bedroom to do it. I could have cried. The old me would have lifted her up and carried her in. I would have lowered her to the bed and-

"Are you okay?"

I nodded, determined to get her in my bed and out of her clothes as quickly as possible. I was afraid she might change her mind before I could make her see the rightness of this.

The rightness of us.

I was in the chair and tugging her onto my lap before she could blink. I didn't trust her not to make a run for it before we got started again.

I couldn't risk it.

She was just that skittish.

And I was going to find out why.

Just as soon as I let out ten years of untapped lust on her delicious body.

Hell, it was going to take a hell of a lot longer than one night to slow me down. But I could get started on easing the ache inside me only Tabby could sooth.

I could hardly wait to get my hands on her.

Tabby let out a soft yip as I squeezed her, rolling us rapidly into the bedroom. I'd gotten adept at buzzing around the lower level since I moved in. Soon, enough I'd be using a walker. Then, I'd be walking with a cane. And then, without.

I decided the first thing I would do when I could walk again was pick her up and carry her around. Maybe pick an advanced level position to try out. Or two.

Or ten.

Up against a wall sounded good. Or bent over a table. Or just standing in the middle of the room with her touching her toes.

Tabby stood up before I could show off by lifting her to the bed. I hopped on and reached for her. She came willingly, but she looked so shy. So nervous.

I hated the thought that she was afraid of me. Or was she afraid of sex? Something was up, but I couldn't figure it out. I thought she might have had bad lovers in the past. Maybe she didn't know how much pleasure a considerate partner could give her.

Well, she was about to find out.

I smiled grimly. I was determined to make her forget every other guy she'd had. I'd blot out the memory of them, just the way she eradicated the thought of any other girl for me.

I wasn't letting her out this bed until she'd come at least five or six times.

She was warm and soft and sweet as I pulled her into my arms and rolled her beneath me.

I groaned as our bodies tangled on the bedspread. I cupped her head, letting myself take all the time I wanted with this. It was just a kiss. But one of sweet surrender.

Tabby was giving in. And doing it so sweetly it made my insides ache.

Soon enough I busied my hands with her clothes. It felt like I'd waited forever. Hell, I kind of *had* waited forever. I was eager to say the least, as I started undressing her again.

Finally that top came all the way off. Then her bra. This was it. The moment I'd been dreaming of since I was a horny teenager with dreams of a naked Tabitha Peterson dancing in my head.

I stopped, realizing there was another bra underneath it. She wasn't naked yet dammit. I would have said something but Tabby looked mortified. I didn't stop though.

I just unhooked the other one.

All my breath came out in a whoosh as my eyes feasted on her naked flesh. Two glorious globes of epic proportions. Gravity defying mounds of soft pink flesh, topped with big hard nipples that were a dusky red.

Holy hell, the woman was perfect. Beyond perfect. My eyes almost bugged out of my head, trying to see everything at once. Her tiny waist. Her sweetly rounded belly.

And those tits. Those magnificent, epic tits.

She crossed her wrists, covering her breasts with her hands. But her chest was so big that her hands didn't begin to hide her lush curves.

A good thing too.

"Let me see you Tabby..."

I reached for her, gently pulling her arms away. I cupped her beautiful breasts in my hands. Oh God. Hot, soft silk. They felt so delicious in my palms that I let out a moan.

"Hmmmffff.... Jesus Tabby... so good... so perfect..."

Then I lowered my head, unable to resist pulling a nipple into my mouth. She tasted so sweet, like honey and cinnamon and vanilla. She was the dessert to end all desserts.

Basically she was my own personal sticky bun.

Oh yeah, I was going to busy with this for a while.

A good long while.

I closed my eyes in bliss and went to town.

TABBY

h my God..."

I held my breath, afraid to look at him. Gabe had just pulled my second bra off. He hadn't said anything about my freakishly large breasts.

He hadn't made a sound.

Not until the moment I was completely exposed to him.

Then he'd groaned and lowered his head to me, gently pushing my hands away. Now he was kissing me. But not my lips.

No, he was kissing me *there.*

Gabe was like a starving man, licking and sucking my nipples like they were the tastiest things on Earth. I gasped as the sensations overwhelmed me. His lips felt good on my breasts. So good that I was forgetting how embarrassed I was to have him see me like this.

I'd been self-conscious about my breasts ever since I hit puberty. They'd come in early. And kept coming. And coming.

The boys had never left me alone after that.

I knew I was a freak. Abnormally top heavy. Unnatural.

But Gabe didn't seem to mind.

"Fuck, you are perfect... so beautiful, Tabby..."

Beautiful? Me?

I knew he was just being nice. I looked cheap. Like I had ridiculously oversized fake boobs. They got in the way constantly. It seemed like everyone was always looking at them.

And everyone commented on them too.

This was the first time I'd ever let anyone touch me. Touch *them.* He couldn't know that. Couldn't know how vulnerable I felt. And yet he was holding me like I was precious.

Like my naked breasts were the most amazing thing that he'd ever in his life.

Minutes passed and he was still at it. He had not lost steam. He had not lifted his head once. Not even to kiss my lips.

He didn't realize how close I was to losing my mind.

I lay there, writhing on the bed while Gabe devoured me. He ate me up, burning me with the fire in his mouth, his hot hands and wet tongue. I felt a need so strong that it made my mind go blank, until I was just one big nerve ending.

He murmured to me, sucking my nipples hard now. Kneading and stroking them as he used his tongue to tease the sensitive points again and again. All my doubts were gone.

Gabe definitely did not think I was a freak.

Or if he did, he really, really liked freaks.

"God Tabby! You are fucking amazing... I have to- Jesus- I want to take these off now, okay?"

He was tugging at my jeans, his fingers sliding between my legs and rubbing me through the thin denim that covered my mound. My hips jerked in response. I let out a low moan, startled by the sound of my own voice.

The way he was touching me... it was making me so hot. So horny. I finally understood what the boys had been after all those years. And for the first time, I didn't blame them one bit.

I'd never felt anything like it.

I nodded and he exhaled in obvious relief, pressing a quick kiss to my lips before he started undoing my jeans. I felt heavy, like I was made out of lead. I wiggled a bit as he slid my jeans down my legs. He pulled my boots off and I heard them hit the floor.

I felt like I was dreaming.

Like it wasn't real.

But then his fingertips were sliding up my bare legs and he was telling me I was so beautiful, that I was driving him crazy, that he wanted me so bad.

That he had always wanted me.

I lost all my will to resist him in that moment. I'd already given in to Gabe inside my head. But now I surrendered in my heart.

He pulled me against him and we both moaned at the contact. I was exposed to him, wearing just the thin cotton of my panties. He kissed me before leaning up on one shoulder to pull his shirt off. Then I was back in his arms, my chest against his.

Skin to skin.

His chest was hot and hard and smooth. The crinkly hairs in the middle tickled my sensitive breasts in the most amazing way. He rubbed against me and the friction made us both gasp with pleasure.

"My God, Tabby... how can you feel this good?"

Gabe buried his face in my neck and kissed me there, sending shivers all over my body. He gripped my thigh and lifted it up and over his hip. I was wrapped around him now, open and exposed to him. His jeans were bulging at the front, his hardness pressing against me. He started to move, curling his hips up and into me.

I gasped at the pressure of him against my center. That was exactly where I wanted it. It was like he knew just how to touch me. Just how to move.

He lowered his head to my nipples again.

"I can't get enough of these..."

I had my hands in his hair, my head tossing back and forth. He cursed as I rocked against him.

"Tabby- fuck- I don't think I can wait."

I stared at him, breathless. He wanted to do it. Now.

And he had no idea I was a virgin.

I wasn't even scared anymore. I didn't care. I just wanted him to stay on top of me. To keep doing what he was doing. To show me everything.

I wanted more.

"Okay."

He grunted as he slid to the side, pulling his pants off. He reached for a condom, giving me a rueful smile.

"You're not on the pill, are you?"

I shook my head.

"No. Is that bad?"

"It's okay, sweetheart. I just want to feel every inch of you."

I blushed, feeling cold without him. My eyes grew wide as he tugged his shorts down and his cock sprang free. It was huge. Hard and curved towards his stomach. The tip glistened as he gripped the shaft, rolling the condom down.

"You're so... big."

He grinned at me, reaching for my panties.

"It's okay sweetie. I promise, I'll fit."

I nodded shakily, reminding myself that this was Gabe. It was Gabe's cock. Gabe's body. He cared about me. This wasn't just some pervy guy pawing at me and wanting to get off.

"I have to taste you. Hmmm..."

My mouth opened in surprise as he lowered his head between my thighs, lapping eagerly at my pussy. A shock ran through my body as he used his finger to slip just inside my lips.

"Hmmm... you are so delicious…"

I felt wild as he toyed with me, my hips moving unconsciously. He shook his head.

"Unfff... God you're so hot. I'm sorry. I promise I will do a better job of this later."

Then he was on top of me again. I felt his cock pushing against my entrance. It felt hot and slick and very, very big. I whimpered as the feeling of him pushing me open overwhelmed me. And then he slipped just inside.

"Oh God..."

He shifted his position above me, pushing up onto his shoulder. I was breathing in little gasps as he lifted one of my legs and held it. Then he pushed forward.

"Unnffff... yes... open up for me..."

I closed my eyes, feeling him stretch me open. He was a few inches inside me. It didn't hurt though. He felt so hot and so big.

So real.

It was finally happening. Everything people had thought I did. I was doing it.

We were doing.

"You're so tight, Tabby... Jesus!" He groaned and slid a little bit further inside me. "Baby, try and relax, I don't want to hurt you."

He pulled out a little and pushed back in. That's when I felt it. Something inside me gave way. It stung, like scraping your knee. Except, it was inside me.

Gabe froze above me, staring down at me. His eyes widened.

"Tabby... Christ- sweetheart, are you a virgin?"

GABE

My cock felt like it was encased in hot, living silk.

Wrapped up like a gift on Christmas morning. Only, it was Tabitha who was the gift.

And I was the first one to open it.

“Tabby… fuck... please... please talk to me..."

I was barely inside her, but I was holding back. She felt so good- too good- but I was afraid to hurt her. I was pretty sure the girl underneath me was a virgin. How the hell that was possible was beyond me.

"Is this your first time?"

She nodded, not meeting my eyes. That was all it took though. I moaned in ecstasy. No wonder she was so snug, so tight. A perfect fit in every way.

And she was all mine.

It blew my mind right then and there. I was the first to touch her. To feel this exquisite body of hers up close. No one had ever so much as put a hand on this gorgeous woman before me.

And no one else ever would.

Just like that, I felt it. It was like a hammer dropped. Like a ship cresting a wave in a storm. The certainty that she was the one for me washed over me. Tabby was it. She was the only one. I'd never even thought about settling down before. Falling in love.

But Tabby had let me in. I was the first. And it changed me.

"You should have told me, Tabby. I would have taken more time- hmmfff-"

Fuck, I was an ass. I should have taken an hour to prepare her. To lick her sweet pussy until she was moaning in pleasure, as desperate for me as I was for her.

I should have taken as long as it took to ease inside her. But it was too late now. I was already partway in and I didn't think there was any force on this planet that would be able to get me to leave.

Not a tsunami. Not an earthquake. Not even a tornado.

Not a Goddamn nuclear explosion.

I pulled out a little, leaving just the tip inside her. "I'm sorry, Tabby." And then I drove myself into her. She cried out and I flinched. But I couldn't have stopped if I had tried to. And I sure as hell wasn't trying.

I was in. Inside the sweetest, tightest, most desirable woman on God's green Earth. I felt like the angels were all singing as her body hugged my cock, quivering and undulating around me.

If I wasn't careful, I was going to come.

Soon.

My balls twitched and I held back a curse. Tabby's eyes were closed tight. Her beautiful face twisted in pain.

"Are you alright? Fuck, I'm so sorry, Tabby-"

Her eyes opened and she looked at me. She nodded, swallowing back tears and my heart broke a little bit. I could see she was trying to be brave.

My feisty, tough girl had been a virgin. And she had given herself to me. I wasn't going to waste it.

"Yes. I'm alright."

I groaned with relief and pleasure as I started to move. She gasped and I froze. "Am I hurting you?" She shook her head and I felt her body bear down on me. I grunted and drove into her again.

I tried to be gentle. I swear that I tried. But I couldn't stop. I had to have her- to fuck her- hard. I needed to be as far inside her as I could get. I needed to screw her into the bed. The wall. The floor.

"Tabby- fuck, I'm going to come!"

It came out of nowhere. My balls were throbbing as they unloaded up my shaft. I let out a roar as my cock exploded with white lightning, pulsing deep inside her. My body lit up like a Christmas tree as I shot load after load into the rubber.

I collapsed forward, realizing she hadn't finished. I had to make that up to her. As soon as I could move again.

Jesus Christ, that was the hardest I'd come in my life!

Not even close.

I reached down to grip the base of my cock, holding the condom as I pulled out. I was still hard, but I didn't want to freak her out with how much I'd come. Thankfully, I had a wastebasket and tissues nearby. I wrapped it all up without her noticing.

That sucker was *full.*

Tabby was laying perfectly still beside me. I turned and pulled her into my arms, moaning as her amazing breasts smashed against my chest. So much soft, feminine goodness. It was almost too much.

Just like that, I felt my balls started filling up again.

I held her face, staring into her beautiful eyes. She looked so soft and dreamy, and I hadn't even gotten started on her. I still needed to make her come. I wanted to hear her squeal. About a hundred times. And that was just tonight.

I smiled and rubbed my thumb over her lip.

"How do you feel?"

She blushed.

"I'm good. I just- I guess I should go."

I tightened my grip around her waist.

"Oh, hell no. You're not going *anywhere*."

She blinked at me, looking confused.

"But aren't you- done?"

I growled and bit her lower lip. She wiggled a little bit in my arms. I slid my hands down to her juicy ass and squeezed.

"You think I'm satisfied with *that*? Honey, that was barely the tip of the iceberg."

"It was?"

"Hell, yes! It was amazing, don't get me wrong. But I plan to have you six ways from Sunday before the night is over."

She looked shocked. She should. I grinned and rolled her to her back, scooting her up the bed so I could get at my prize. The prize I'd been after since before I had hair on my chest.

I guided her silky thighs apart and rested them on my shoulders. Her sweetness was right there, ready for the tasting. I took a good look at her puffy little lips before pressing my mouth against her.

It was pussy eating time.

TABBY

"What are you- oh!"

I stared at the ceiling in shock as Gabe slowly licked my pussy bottom to top. He used his tongue to make long slow strokes. I held perfectly still as he tasted me, over and over again. I didn't know what I was supposed to do.

I'd thought we were finished. I was relieved that it was over to be honest. Not that I didn't like it. I was just glad I hadn't done anything weird or embarrassing.

In fact, I'd liked sex more than I'd thought I would.

It was... nice.

Even though it had hurt a little. I guess that was normal the first time. I'd been worried about what he'd think about that too, hoping he might not even notice.

But Gabe seemed more than happy that I'd been a virgin. He seemed ecstatic. And now he was doing things to me that were even more intimate.

He was so close to me, his fingers slid up my body to play with my nipples as he pulled my clit into his mouth. I arched off the bed, shocked by the intensity of the feeling. My fingers reached down, tangling in his soft, wavy hair.

"Hmmm... that's so nice baby... you taste so good..."

He started doing something wicked with his tongue- flicking it hard and fast against me. He pinched my nipples gently and moaned. I felt the vibrations against my pussy. Almost like he was enjoying this as much as I was.

But that was impossible. Because I'd never felt anything like it. It felt like the best thing on Earth.

It felt like heaven.

"That's it Tabby... reach for it..."

I screamed as a wave of pleasure crashed over me.

He didn't even take a pause to breath, he just kept going. Licking and touching me, coaxing aftershock after aftershock until the orgasm finally started to fade.

I was barely aware of where I was as I lay there. Gabe smiled at me and reached to the bedside table. I blinked as I realized what he was doing.

He was rolling another condom over his shaft.

His thick, enormous, already hard again shaft.

"What are you doing, Gabe? You want to do that... Again?"

He grinned at me and rolled me to face him. He nuzzled my neck. "Yes, I want to do that again. Is that alright?" I nodded shyly and his smile faded, replaced by a serious and purposeful look. His eyes even looked like a darker shade of green. His face was a mask of concentration as he stared between my legs.

I felt him pressing against me, then he groaned as he watched himself sink inside me.

"Jesus Tabby... it's not... It's not supposed to feel this good."

"It's not?"

He shook his head, closing his eyes.

"No, sweetheart. It's not."

He was silent as he started to move, easing deeper inside me with every stroke. For a while, the only sounds were his harsh breathing and our bodies moving together. I was tender, but he was careful and it didn't hurt. It felt almost too good, like he said.

I was even more sensitive after all the attention he'd given me. And what he'd done with his mouth. I felt myself clench down on him, close to coming again.

Whatever his intentions towards me might be, Gabe definitely was a considerate lover. More than considerate. Generous. Passionate. Wildly eager.

He wasn't faking how he felt. I knew it. He wanted me.

Every inch of me.

He lowered his head to my breasts and started kissing them, not stopping his long, deep strokes. He worked his cock in and out of me, slowly picking up the pace.

When he looked up at me again, his eyes went right through me. Right to my soul. I was frozen in place, unable to look away.

The look in his eyes was so intense, so real, it was almost painful.

"Tabitha..."

He growled and pulled me hard against him, his mouth capturing mine. Our tongues intertwined as his hips circled, faster and faster. He swallowed the sound as I cried out, my head flung back as my entire body shattered into light.

But I wasn't alone.

Gabe shattered with me.

I *felt* him shatter.

He let out a low grunt as he jerked, his body slamming into mine. Once. Twice. And then he was still, other than the slight tremors that shook us both.

He held me for the longest time, raining soft kisses on my face, my neck.

It was a half an hour later when his breathing had evened out into sleep. I slipped from the bed and started pulling my clothes on. Every cell in my body wanted to stay in bed with him. I felt good, relaxed.

I felt like I was doing something wrong by sneaking out but I couldn't be here in the morning.

I stood in the doorway and looked back at him. Gabe looked so handsome tangled up in the sheets, his face soft and peaceful. I couldn't stop myself as I watched him for a moment. Then I snuck out into the early morning light.

GABE

I woke up smiling. I had done it. I had made Tabby mine. We'd made love twice, and each time had been specfuckingtacular. I was the first to have her. And I was going to be the last.

I'd finally found the woman for me. And I was going to tell her so. Right after I made her squeal with pleasure again.

That glorious feeling lasted about thirty seconds.

The bed beside me was cold.

I looked around, realizing she'd left me. I scowled. Why the hell had she done that? Then I remembered how shy Tabby was about some things. Maybe she didn't want my mom to see her.

But that was bullshit, man.

Tabby was my woman now dammit. There was no need to sneak around. I decided I would tell her so, too.

I'd put a Goddamn cowbell on her if I had to. Or a bow, with a tag that said my name. Or a homing device.

Or a ring.

I sat up straight in bed.

I was seriously considering marrying Tabitha. I could see us getting older together. She'd be sexy as hell at 30. And 40. Hell, I'd still think she was beautiful no matter how many wrinkles or gray hairs she got.

And she'd give me such beautiful children...

Well, that was a first. I'd never thought past getting a girl into bed before, and rarely even had to think about that. Girls had never required any effort for me.

Well, except for *her.*

Tabby had been damn near impossible to get until now. And she was continuing to be a pain in my ass by sneaking out on me. She'd deprived me of morning sex too. But I was willing to be understanding now that she was mine.

After all, she had given me the best sex of my life.

The best by about a million.

A zillion.

I took a shower and got dressed. I had a lot to think about. The rest of my life with Tabby for starters. My mother had left out some juice and a bagel. I shook my head, wondering what my woman would say about that.

I could hear Tabby scolding me now. 'Empty carbs', she'd say. Or that I needed protein. Or that I should eat an orange instead of drinking it.

I grinned. She'd be here soon. Then I could relax and let her fuss over me. I'd smile and nod and as soon as my mother was out of the house, I'd pounce.

I was going to spend my day in bed today. But not resting. Oh hell no, I was going to spend it getting all the exercise a healthy boy needed. And Tabby was going to be screaming my name in pleasure the whole damn time.

"Gabe? Your aid is here."

I glanced sharply towards the stairs. My mother stood there, looking uncertain. Her hands were tugging on each other. I was about to ask her what was wrong when I saw it.

Or rather, I saw *her.*

She was... not Tabby.

A middle-aged woman stood behind my mother. She wore a nurse uniform and sensible shoes. She was exactly what you thought of when you thought of a home caregiver.

But she was not my caregiver. I already had one. And I needed her. I needed Tabby.

Where the fuck was Tabitha?

"Where is she?"

I wheeled over to the stairs.

"Gabe, this is Annie. She's here from the service."

I nodded my head to the woman and said good morning. There was no reason to be rude. Especially, since she was about to be out on her ass. "It's nice to meet you Annie but I already have an aid." I whipped my head to face my mother. *"Where is she?"*

"I'll- I'll go find out. Annie, would you wait upstairs with me while we sort this out?"

"Fine. You do that. I'll try Tabitha."

I picked up my phone and dialed her cell. I sat in my chair, staring out the back window, trying to get my temper under control.

"Hello?"

I heard the sleep in her voice. It only made me angrier. She was in bed! She should have just stayed here with me!

"Where are you?"

"Gabe?"

Her voice sounded worried. Good. She should be fucking worried. She'd scared the hell out of me twice and it wasn't even 9 o'clock!

"The service called and told me they found a replacement. I told them it wasn't necessary- I told them never mind but it was too late."

I closed my eyes. She hadn't run out on me again. It was just a mix up.

"Anyway Gabe, it's good for you to have backup. And I don't think I should do-"

She went silent.

"What Tabby?"

She sighed.

"I don't think I should do... both."

I clenched the phone.

"You won't take care of me?"

I knew it was a low blow but I took it anyway. It hurt like hell that she was making this an 'either or' situation.

"I will! I want to help you Gabe. Anyway I can. And I need the job. But what happened last night... it's not right. And it's a breach of my contract."

I grit my teeth.

"So you'll be my girlfriend, or my nurse. Not both."

"Girlfriend? You want me to be- your girlfriend?"

I realized my hand was squeezing the phone again and forced myself to relax. I was going to break it. My hands had always been exceptionally strong.

"Yes, Tabby. What the fuck did you think we were doing last night?"

"I don't know. I thought maybe that was-"

"What? You thought it was what?"

"I thought that was what you wanted." A pause. "Just that."

"No. That's not all I want. Not by a long shot."

I wanted to scream at her for thinking that. Only, maybe she was right. I *had* just wanted to roll around with her at first. Not just once or twice. I'd wanted to have her as much as possible, but I hadn't thought about much past that.

Yeah, I wanted as much sex as a growing boy could handle.

But with every minute I spent with her, I wanted more than just sex.

Much more.

"Oh."

I could hear the shyness in her voice. I nodded to myself. That was better. She was going to be a good girl.

It wasn't her fault she was new at this.

"Are you coming over here?"

She hesitated.

"I have to work tonight. They want me to come in early for lunch too and- well, you're covered anyway today, aren't you?"

"Yeah. I'm covered. Tomorrow?"

"I told them I would come in tomorrow but-"

"I know. It's one or the other."

I swallowed hard, realizing I was going to have to get out of this damn chair if I wanted her with me more than a few snatched hours at a time. If I wanted her with me as a woman, not a nurse.

Not an employee.

She said goodbye and hung up. I sat there for the longest time, just thinking. I heard my mother clear her throat and looked up. She must have caught the end of the conversation.

"Is she coming?"

"Tomorrow."

She nodded.

"Alright son. Is there anything you need before I- before Annie takes over?"

"Yes. Get me my cane."

Her eyes got wide.

"But you are supposed to do physical therapy for at least another week before-"

I gave my mom a look of pure steel and she threw her hands up. She might be tough, but I was even more stubborn and we both knew it. She went upstairs and came back with a black wood cane and a folding silver walker.

She snapped the walker into place and adjusted the height.

I frowned at it, shaking my head.

"I'm not using that damn thing. It's worse than the chair."

"It's more stable than the cane. Just for the first few days Gabe." She arched an eyebrow at me. "Start with this. Please. You can put it away if Tabby comes over."

I glared at her. Obviously, she had caught which way the wind was blowing. But she was implying that Tabitha wasn't coming back.

"*When* Tabby comes over. Just for today, okay?"

I gave her a curt nod, knowing she was right. I spent the rest of the day doing my exercises and experimenting with the walker and the cane. The walker *was* more stable. It was almost like using a crutch that didn't wobble. I used it to put a bit of pressure on my leg, increasing it slightly until it hurt, then backing off again.

I nodded to myself. I *was* going to be walking in no time.

And after that, I was going to chase my woman down.

TABBY

"Good morning."

I smiled tentatively at Gabe. He looked impossibly handsome, stretched out on the couch with a book. I noticed his chair was gone.

"Oh, you graduated!"

I frowned, tilting my head. I'd only been gone a day. What was going on?

"Did you get the go ahead for the walker?"

He tapped a cane leaning against the couch.

"No walker."

"Gabe... are you sure that's a good idea?"

He just raised an eyebrow at me.

"I thought you were just my aid. Not my doctor. And not my girlfriend. Right?"

"I'm sorry about yesterday. I told you-"

He went back to reading his book and I stopped, staring at him in shock. He was ignoring me completely. Where was the guy who was all over me, chasing me all over the damn town?

I'd stayed up all night, talking to Jackie in Paris. She was thrilled that I'd finally lost my V card. Beyond that though, I hadn't told anyone else. Or told Jacks exactly how scared I was about my feelings for Gabe.

I turned away and started organizing his pills. I noticed his pain meds were also gone. What the heck had happened here yesterday?

I was about to ask him when I caught him staring at me. He looked away so fast, that I knew he was up to something. Was he only pretending to ignore me?

Either way, I didn't like it.

But if he was going to keep his distance, so would I. I knew it was for the best. Until I didn't work for him, anything else was off limits. And after that, one or both of us would be long gone from this town anyway.

The fantasy of the two of us as more than friends was pretty much a lost cause.

"What are you going to do? Next, I mean?"

He set his book down and looked at me.

"That sounds like a dangerously personal question, Miss."

I rolled my eyes. I couldn't tell if he was being funny, or if he was pissed off at me. Probably both. He was annoyed with me for telling him no funny business anymore, that much was obvious.

Gabe definitely did not like it when he didn't get his way. And he wanted me in his bed.

I blushed, thinking about what we'd done together, less than 36 hours ago.

What we'd done *twice.*

"Never mind. Sorry I asked."

"If you must know, I was thinking of opening up my own place. Maybe a cafe somewhere down the coast."

I looked at him, surprised. Cooking? Gabe? Serving coffee?

But... it sounded nice.

"Oh." I nodded to myself, not sure what to say. "I'll be right back with your lunch."

I put a tray together and was setting it down when he came out of the bathroom. He was on two feet, standing tall but favoring one leg. It was impossible to ignore the grimace on his gorgeous face.

"Are you okay? Let me get the chair-"

"No. I got this."

He made it across the room without looking too bad. But he moaned as he sat down on the couch. I was by his side in an instant.

"You are doing too much, too soon!"

He shrugged.

"Maybe if you rubbed it..."

I bit my lip and nodded, pushing the tray out of the way. He leaned back and watched me as I sat beside him.

"We should really do this in shorts."

He shook his head, making an odd sound. I shrugged and reached for his leg.

"It won't be as effective."

His thigh muscles felt good under my hand. Thick and strong. He hadn't lost much tone since his injury. That was good...

He grunted and I looked up.

"Does that hurt?"

He shook his head and I went back to focusing on what I was doing.

It was important to get the blood moving with a brisk rub but not to overstimulate the tissues. Adding the magnesium and castor oil would only increase the benefits.

I tried another angle that had me kneeling on the floor between his thighs. I was so focused on what I was doing that it took me a moment to realize how heavily he was breathing. Gabe let out a low growl and I froze. I just happened to glance down at that moment.

Gabe was hard.

Not just a little hard either.

His massive cock was pushing up, clearly outlined against his worn in jeans. I could see the thick, long shape of it. I could feel it giving off *actual heat.*

To call it a bulge would be an understatement. It wasn't even a tent.

It was a mountain.

"Gabe!"

His eyes were closed.

"Hmmm... that's nice Tabby... keep going..."

"But- you're- I can't!"

He cracked one eye and looked at me.

"I'm what?"

"You're erect!"

He just shrugged like it was no big deal.

"It's natural."

"What is that supposed to mean?"

"It means I'm relaxed. Nothing more. You know, when you are a nurse, this sort of thing is going to happen. Old guys. Sponge baths. Teenagers. Guys get wood. It's natural."

He leaned back and closed his eyes again.

"*That's* what I meant."

I was still between his legs on the floor. I felt stupid. But he was right- it wasn't that crazy that a massage would create... arousal. It didn't mean it was because of me.

Slowly, I reached out and started rubbing him again. He made a low sound of appreciation. Then another.

Then he groaned like I was doing him!

"Hmmmffff... fuck, that feels good, baby..."

"Gabe!"

My cheeks were bright red. He was making sounds like he did when we were in bed together. When we'd- when he'd- oh!

I was so embarrassed I almost left the room. But I wouldn't be doing my job then would I? He had to eat and take his pills now.

And I couldn't leave him here alone. I was getting paid to be here.

Gabe knew it too.

He was trying to prove a point or something. Prove that we couldn't undo what had happened between us.

But all he'd done was make me feel like a whore.

I stood up and walked across the room, trying to hide my tears. I put his pills into a small cup and waited until I heard the sounds of him eating. Then I carried the cup over and set it down.

I didn't meet his eyes. I didn't sit down. I went to the bathroom like a coward. I splashed cold water on my face, not looking at the mirror. I was afraid of what I would see. I sat on the edge of the tub, praying for strength.

And waited.

And waited.

When I came out Gabe was standing by the sliding doors. He was using the walker this time though, keeping his injured leg slightly bent. I frowned, realizing he must have been showing off with the cane earlier.

For me.

I shook my head. He didn't need to do that. He knew what he was. Who he was. He was strong.

Not like me.

I still had everything to prove to this town. The world.

Myself.

"You okay? I thought you fell in."

He was facing me, using the walker to come closer. I skittered around him to get his tray. I had meant to ask him why he was off his pain meds, but I didn't.

I wasn't a very good caregiver.

Not today.

I managed to avoid talking to him the rest of the day. He tried. He even tried to touch my arm when I brought him a protein shake a few hours later.

I exhaled in relief when I heard his mother come in a little early. This hell could be over a little sooner then. I could escape and lick my wounds. I wonder what advice Jackie would have for me now.

The moment the clock struck five, I ran.

GABE

I stared out the window, my jaw clenching as Tabitha ran down the path outside toward the street. She was running away from me. Because I was an idiot. A fool.

A fool who couldn't control his urges. Even when I'd told her I would.

I saw her slide into her car and wipe furiously at her cheeks.

Shit. She was crying.

I felt like the biggest creep in the world. And I knew she was not coming back here. There was no way. I'd fucking blown it.

And then the best, or worst, thing in the world happened. Good for me. Bad for her.

I watched as she turned the ignition again and again.

Her piece of shit car wouldn't start.

I grabbed my jacket and keys and went outside. The walker was a hell of a lot easier than the cane, especially on uneven surfaces. I could keep most of the weight off my thigh. Or if I was feeling strong, I could just use the walker as backup.

I stood up straight, determined not to look like an old man.

"Tabby."

She had her arms crossed where she rested them on the front wheel. Her shoulders were shaking slightly. She wasn't crying prettily, for attention. She was bawling her damn eyes out.

I hated seeing her like this. Seeing how badly she'd been hurt by the world.

And I'd made it worse.

I knocked on the glass and she jumped.

"Hey."

She blinked at me, wiping her tears away. She covered her face with her jacket, blotting her cheeks. Then she rolled down the window.

"It stopped running again?"

She nodded, her pretty face flushed and pink from crying. I decided then and there to get her a new car. Hell, I'd give her mine until the new one came.

Right now though, I saw an opportunity to get her alone.

"I'll give you a ride."

She was about to refuse me when she thought better of it. She said 'okay' in a small voice. I had to stifle a laugh when she locked the door. Like anyone would steal that heap of junk.

"Are you working tonight?"

She shook her head numbly. I could tell she had had more than enough. I wasn't going to push her to talk about us. She needed some TLC.

Luckily, I had plenty of that to go around. At least, where she was concerned. I got into my car and was able to get the walker into the back without her help.

Damn, the stupid thing might be ugly, but it was versatile.

I started driving towards the water. Tabby looked around as we pulled onto the coast road.

"Where are you going? I thought you were driving me home."

"I thought we could both use some air." I smiled at her. "And something to eat."

"Gabe..."

"I'm not taking no for an answer, Tabby."

She chewed her lip and sat back, staring out the window. I drove all the way down to the edge of town and past it. One town over was my favorite place to eat. The best damn beach shack on the Eastern Seaboard. And it was open off season.

This was the kind of place I wanted to open up. But... someplace a little warmer.

I was pretty sure they didn't have places like this anywhere else on Earth. I should know, I'd traveled enough in the service. But more than anything along the rocky coast line, this little lobster shack made me think of home.

Tabby was quiet as we walked inside. I was really getting the hang of the walker. It was better than the damn chair, that was for sure.

I liked moving on my own steam.

Still, if I was normal- if I was whole- I'd have my arm around her. Hell, I might carry her everywhere. She'd be a nice little bundle.

I grinned. As soon as I could walk again, I'd have to try that.

The smell of wood polish and lemon and fresh seafood hit us the second we were inside the door. It wasn't packed, but it was always busy, even in the off-season.

The place was simple but classy. Or at least, *classic.*

Sure, there were some nets and buoys on the wall, but it was kept to a minimum. The place was warm and inviting, with dark polished wood and comfortable looking booths lining a wall that overlooked the sea.

"I love this place."

She looked up at me, her huge dark eyes surprised. Since I'd been in the chair this whole time, I'd been looking up at her instead. I realized this was the first time I'd been taller than her since high school.

Well, except when we were laying down.

She looked good from up here. Small, and sweet. And tasty.

"I've never been here."

I shook my head.

"Come on. You're gonna love it."

We were seated by the wall of windows overlooking the large deck. It was closed for the season, but luckily, they stayed open indoors all winter. It was the only seafood place around here that did.

But since they were famous for their hot chowder, they made it work.

We got our menus and ordered. Well, I ordered, and Tabby gave me looks and clucked her tongue to convey her opinion. I ordered and then unordered a soda. I got her a white wine and two pound lobster. She made a noise and I amended it to a one and a half pound.

I got a two pounder for myself.

And steamers. And sides. And a cup of chowder for us both.

As soon as the waitress left, Tabby leaned forward.

"Gabe! It's too expensive!"

I just smiled. I could afford to spoil her. And I was just getting started.

"Haven't you had lobster before?"

She nodded.

"I've tasted it. But I never had a whole one."

"You're going to love it. Just relax Tabby."

She looked so worried. It was freaking adorable.

"I don't want you spending all your money on me."

I leaned back in my seat.

"I did well for myself, sweetie. I saved my money. You don't have to worry about that."

"But you want to open a business. That's expensive."

I grinned. I liked this side of her. She cared about my future. But I could afford to take my woman out for lobster. And more. I was going to spoil her rotten, whether she liked it or not.

"I'm good. Stop worrying."

She chewed her lip while the waitress brought our drinks.

"Is this what you meant? When you said you wanted to open your own place?"

I nodded, taking a sip of my water.

"Yeah, but down coast. Maybe as far as the Carolinas."

Her eyes were wide.

"I've thought of... going down there. Or west."

"California?"

She shrugged her slender shoulders. I did my best to ignore her cleavage. It was a nice view sitting across from her like this, and I wasn't talking about the ocean.

"Maybe."

"You really want to leave don't you?"

"Yes."

I looked away, then back at her. I knew my heart was in my eyes. She saw it too.

"Maybe we could leave this place together. Did you ever think about that?"

She was staring at the table.

"I try not to- think about things that are out of reach. It's easier that way."

I grabbed her hand and squeezed it. I waited until she looked at me.

"I'm not out of reach. I'm right here"

Her mouth opened and I stared at her soft lips.

"You're the one who keeps pulling away."

"I don't know the rules, Gabe. I've never done this before. Any of it."

I grinned at her wolfishly.

"I know. And I'm damn lucky to be the one who gets to teach you."

She blushed and I felt a shot of lust go straight to my groin.

"I didn't just mean that."

She nodded softly.

"I know."

The food came soon after and I had fun feeding her, and watching her savor the food. She was in awe of it, the freshness and quality. They cooked everything from scratch here, and with the simplest ingredients.

No farmed fish, or GMO corn. And they'd even started using organic ingredients. Old Betty came out and said hi, and told us all about it.

She beamed with pride as I introduced Tabby as my girlfriend.

"Wow, you really must come here a lot."

I laughed.

"Yeah, I do. Or I used to. I still get a Christmas card every year."

"Everybody loves you. They always have."

I stared at her, realizing how good I'd had it. I had been kind of a golden boy. In this town anyway. I never had an enemy. I never had something I wanted and couldn't get.

Except her.

But what I really wanted to know was if she loved me. If she thought she ever could.

Because what I knew, beyond a shadow of a doubt, was that I was in love with her.

"Come on, let's stretch our legs."

I gave Gabe a startled look. It was chilly on the water, but the night was clear. He smiled sheepishly.

"All three of them."

I let out a startled laugh. He really had a funny sense of humor. And I had to admire that he never felt sorry for himself or complained, even with everything he'd gone through. And I knew he must feel cooped up in that house.

"Okay, but not far. You shouldn't overdo it."

He nodded and we started down the walkway to the marina. There was a boardwalk about fifty yards long that led to the docks. It was probably not exactly open to the public, but it also wasn't the sort of place where people locked gates or front doors.

Plus, Gabe seemed to know the area well, and he wasn't concerned at all either.

I decided that if he wasn't concerned, then I wasn't going to be concerned either. I was through worrying about every little thing. So much was out of my control anyway.

Gabe stopped and slid his arm around my waist.

"Are you warm enough?"

I nodded, pulling my zipper up to my neck. It was chilly, but too beautiful to pass up. Besides, I knew he couldn't walk on the sand. So this was the closest he'd gotten to the water in months.

I wasn't going to deprive him of his 'vitamin sea' as he called it.

The man was a water lover, to say the least.

I guess you had to be, if you were going to join the Navy.

"Do you miss it? Being in the service I mean?"

He gave me a swift look.

"I do. I miss the guys. The ocean. The order of everything. But I think the timing was good in a lot of ways. I was ready for a change."

He winked at me.

"And I don't just mean meeting you."

"Meeting?"

"Well, meeting you *again*. It's not like we really had a chance to get to know each other back in high school."

I nodded. I knew what he meant. We'd been separated by so much back then. He cleared his throat.

"I wasn't just after- well, you know."

"Really?"

I cocked an eyebrow at him. I knew he wanted to be with me now- to date me- or at least he said he did. But back then, he was a horny teenager.

"Yeah. I really liked you Tabby." He smiled sheepishly. "You were mysterious. And so beautiful it made my head spin."

"I was?"

"You still are."

"If you say so."

"You seriously don't know the effect you have on men?"

I frowned and looked at my feet. I did that whenever he brought up something that made me uncomfortable.

"I know most guys act like they have a right to touch me. I hate that."

Gabe's hand tightened on my waist. His voice changed, just like that. It was cold. Hard. I shivered, realizing I would never want to piss him off.

"Has anyone touched you Tabby?"

I shook my head. He looked furious. His eyes were blazing.

"No. But- well, plenty have tried. Like at the bar. Nothing more than that."

"You swear to me? I'll be happy to put a beat down on anyone who's hurt you."

"They just grab. That's why I carry pepper spray."

He let out a whoosh of air. The wind blew past us, whipping my hair around my face. We were facing each other at the end of the pier, all the way out on the ocean.

"I'd like to pummel every guy that made you feel uncomfortable."

"I can handle myself, Gabe. I've had to for a long time." I smiled to soften the serious turn our conversation was taking. "But I guess I wouldn't mind if you punched a few of them."

He laughed and smiled at me and then I was in his arms. I could feel the walker between us. He must have too, because he cursed the 'damn thing'. But he didn't stop kissing me.

"God Tabby, you are amazing."

He kissed me until we were both shivering. But not from the cold. From the excitement of almost-first-kisses and honesty and getting to know someone you really liked. Then he stopped, staring down at me in wonder. His knuckles rubbed my cheek tenderly.

"So soft..." He kissed me again. "Let me come home with you, Tabby. I promise I'll be good..."

I laughed.

"That's what I'm afraid of!"

But I nodded in agreement anyway. I couldn't turn back now. I knew I was already lost.

"Okay. Let's go."

GABE

Her house smelled like lemons. That was the first thing I noticed as I stepped into the small house where Tabitha had grown up. The outside was rundown, which was not surprising in this neighborhood, and it was small. But it smelled amazing inside.

Pretty much everything Tabby touched smelled good.

I looked around the cramped living room. It was neatly organized and sparkling clean, but out of date with a floral sofa and chair with doilies on the arm rests. You could tell an old lady had lived here for a long time.

There were no signs that a young girl had lived here, though it was obvious Tabby had been busy. There were boxes along one wall, and what looked like shipping supplies.

That's when it hit me.

She was really leaving.

Leaving this town, and unless I was smart, leaving me.

Not on my watch, dammit.

"Sorry about the mess."

I shook my head.

"It's not messy at all."

"Oh, it is. There are boxes and stuff. I'm just trying to get organized. And make sure I keep the stuff that really mattered to Gran. Things to remember her by."

I watched her hungrily as she shrugged out of her coat. Her plain old shirt stretched over her glorious tits as she pulled off her scarf. She leaned forward and draped it carefully over the back of a chair. Everything she did was so deliberate, so mindful. I let my eyes wander down her long legs and back up again to that delicious ass of hers.

I can't lie, I was wondering if it would be rude to try and fuck her on that old lady couch. It didn't look comfortable but I wasn't sure I could wait for the grand tour.

"Meeeerrrre!"

"Speaking of cranky old things my Gran loved..." She bent down and scratched a scrawny looking kitty behind the ears. I watched as it strolled over to me and immediately leaned into my leg, rubbing itself all over me.

"That's weird. She never does that."

"Animals love me."

It was true. In the service the dogs went nuts when I walked by. It drove the kennel masters crazy. Something about pheromones, most likely.

"Not me. This ungrateful thing only likes me when there is food or body heat involved." She stood there awkwardly while I scratched the cat's head. "Do you want something to drink?"

"No. Do you?"

She bit her lip.

"Do you want to sit down?"

I looked at the couch and back at her.

"That depends."

"On what?"

"How far away your bed is."

"Oh."

The truth was, I wasn't even patient enough to wait for the couch. I reached out for her and pulled her against my chest. I moaned as I felt her curves melt into me.

"Tabby..."

Her voice was shaky when she answered me.

"The bedroom is- just down here."

"Okay. Good." I nodded, relieved she wasn't being too coy about this. "Lead the way."

I followed her down the hallway to a small, almost austere room. There was a picture of a waterfall above the bed, which was covered with a faded pink quilt. No photos. Not the kind of room I imagined a teenage Tabby growing up in.

But that thought barely even registered. Because we were here. In her bedroom. The place I'd fantasized about a thousand times growing up.

Over the past month or so too.

I smiled at her and shut the door behind me. The bed was a twin, but that was fine. She wasn't big. Well, except for her-

"Gabe!"

She squealed as I grabbed her without warning. I was on her in a heartbeat, my hands guiding us both down to the bed. I didn't have time to be polite about this. I needed her.

Now.

"Hmmm... take this off..."

I tugged at her button down insistently. She blinked at me while I worked on her shoes. If she worked on the top, and I started on the bottom, she would be naked faster.

That was the kind of planning we learned in the military. Divide and conquer. Seek and destroy.

Allocate assets where needed.

And I needed those assets. ASAP.

She unbuttoned her shirt and I felt my mouth go dry at the sight of the lace peeking out from underneath. If she ever started wearing fancy lingerie, I might not survive it.

She was already so sexy. So beautiful. So perfect.

And she was mine.

I grinned as her fuzzy little boots hit the floor. Then I was crawling up her body, tugging at her jeans. I kissed her soft belly as I pulled the jeans open, grinning wickedly at her as I gently slid them down. Her shirt was open but she'd left her bra on. I knew she was shy so I didn't say anything.

She wouldn't be shy with me for long.

Then I was on her, my chest pressing down against those luscious breasts of hers.

"Jesus Tabby... you drive me crazy..."

She gasped as I slid one hand between our bodies to stroke her through her panties. "Do you like that Tabby?" She nodded breathlessly as I teased her puffy little lips through the thin cotton.

"Hmmmfff... so soft... take the rest off."

Her eyes were closed as she lay there, still way too covered up for my liking. I needed to see those tits of hers. I wanted to bury my face in her softness and never come out again.

She blushed as she helped me pull the rest of her clothes off of her.

"The first thing I'm going to do when I can walk again is take you up against a wall."

Her eyes got wide and I could tell I had shocked her. I thought she might scold me, or tell me she wasn't going to be around much longer. But she bit her lip instead.

"Well, it's important to have goals."

I let out a startled laugh. She always surprised me. I had a feeling Tabby would keep me on my toes for years to come.

Then she unclasped her bra and I swear I could see heaven as her glorious breasts spilled out. She was only wearing one bra this time. I was glad, but only because it took less time for her to get naked.

My eyes were glued to her chest as I cupped her luscious mounds in both hands. She filled my big palms, and then some. I moaned and gently squeezed them, then lowered my head to get a taste.

I lost myself in her breasts, kneading and stroking and sucking them. If my cock hadn't been so desperate to get out of my pants, I could have spent hours just playing with her delicious body.

As it was, my dick had other ideas.

I groaned and lifted my head, staring down at her as I kicked my shoes off. It was impossible to chose what to do next. Touch her, taste her or take her. I wanted it all, and all at the same time.

I reminded myself that we had all night.

She couldn't exactly sneak out of her own house.

So I started with my lips.

I kissed my way up her body as I unfastened my jeans. I got them open and left them that way. That way it would be easy to free the beast when the time came.

I had to make Tabby come first. In fact, my plan was to make her so delirious with pleasure, she'd never think about leaving me again.

I paused, realizing what I'd just thought. I wanted her for the long-term. I knew that. But it was becoming evident that I wanted even more than that.

I wanted forever.

I was going to marry Tabitha Peterson.

I slid her silky thighs apart and started feasting on my future wife.

TABBY

Something was different. I felt it the moment he positioned himself between my legs. Gabe was so tender, so reverent, it was like he was worshipping me with his mouth and tongue.

He worked me slowly, gently, but also relentlessly.

The way his hands gripped me, holding me firmly as I came, shaking and arching off the bed. The way he didn't stop licking me until I'd peaked again and again.

And when he slid inside me a half an hour later, I saw it in his eyes.

Gabe was looking at me like he owned me. He paused with the tip of his cock against me, his eyes blazing with heat.

"I don't want to wear a condom."

"What?"

"I just want to feel you- just for a little while. I'm clean."

"Oh."

He waited until I nodded. I wanted to feel him too. I knew it was stupid, but I was so relaxed and turned on, I didn't care.

He moaned as he pressed forward, his cock nudging my lips apart as he sank into me.

I gasped at the feel of his bare cock inside me. It felt amazing- so different from the condom. He was so big, and silky and hot. And somehow- more.

He moaned and whispered soft words to me. I was tossing my head so I almost missed it. He said it again. "What?" I stammered.

Gabe stared down at me, pausing the slow and steady circular motion of his hips.

"Do you love me Tabby?"

"I-"

I didn't know what to say. I *had* been in love with him from afar for so long. But he couldn't know that. And this was different.

I'd been so careful to protect myself. How had he figured it out?

"I love you Tabby. Do you love me back?"

I stared up at him. *He loved me?* Gabe flexed his hips, driving his cock deeper and then pulling out again. I cried out, my fingers gripping his shoulders. Then he went still again.

I was close, and he knew it.

"Tabby... tell me. Do you love me?"

"Please Gabe... Oh!"

Something about the immoveable force of his cock was doing strange things to me. He was utterly still, poised halfway inside me. I could feel every inch of him as my body squeezed him, trying to pull him closer.

But he held still, waiting.

Then he pinched my nipple.

"Fine. But I'm keeping you up all night until you say it."

"What?"

I gasped as he shifted back and the cool air hit my skin.

"I'm keeping you up until you admit that you love me back. And it's not going to be fun."

"It's- not?"

He licked his lips and looked over my body.

"No. It's not."

Then he got to work.

I was flat on my back, already on the verge. He told me to close my eyes and I did. Then he covered my eyes with his shirt, tying it behind my head. I reached for him, but found only air.

"Gabe!"

He shushed me and grasped my hands, pressing them down to my sides.

"Behave."

I squirmed and he chuckled. He trailed his fingertips over my skin. He started at my chest and dragged them down over my belly, skimming my hips and thighs until he reached my ankles. Then he did it again.

I whimpered as he blew cold air on my nipples. Then lower, on my belly and thighs. Then on the soles of my feet.

"Gabe..."

"Tell me."

But I couldn't.

I felt him settle beside me and then my torture began in earnest. He played with my nipples for a while before letting his hand slide down to my belly.

He traced the outline of my pussy once, and then again. I moaned as he toyed with my clit before moving his hand away.

My hips jerked, seeking, but not finding the pressure of his fingers.

"Please..."

"Tell me."

"I- I care about you."

"You love me. Say it."

I wanted to say it. But I couldn't.

"Don't be such a coward."

But I was.

So he kept going. I tossed and turned but he held me down, teasing me until I was on the verge of tears. I wanted him so badly, I could have screamed.

When he finally pushed himself inside me again, I did.

He pulled the blindfold off as he rode me, both of us desperate for release. We stared into each others eyes as our animal instincts took over. We rocked wildly until we came together.

Gabe shouted his release as I said his name, my body locking down on his.

It was later when we were curled up on the tiny bed that I made my mistake. I thought he was asleep when I whispered the words into his neck, so softly there was no way he could have heard them.

"I do love you, Gabe."

He squeezed me and smiled without opening his eyes.

"I know."

GABE

She loved me. She did.

I groaned as I slid into her welcoming warmth for the third time. The third time since we'd crawled into her childhood bed. She'd finally admitted it, deep into the night. Now it was early morning and I was making her mine again.

Tabby was mine. This perfect woman was mine.

In a way, it felt like she always had been.

Even if she hadn't known it till now.

"Hmmm you feel so good Tabby... are you close?"

She was silent, wordlessly moaning in that sexy way of hers but it didn't matter. I could feel it. The glorious fluttering that happened when she was about to come. Then when she did, unfff, she'd squeeze me so tight I had no choice but to come with her.

I moaned as my cock started to swell, my balls heavy with seed even though I'd drained them twice. And not just drained. I'd unleashed two big loads already.

Deep inside her.

We hadn't worn a condom once all night.

I hoped she'd get pregnant. Give me lots and lots of babies. Or not. I'd love her even if it was just the two of us growing old together.

Either way though, I was keeping her.

The thought of her belly all big and round with our child was enough to send me over the edge. I could do that. I could make a child with her. I cursed as light shot up through the base of my cock and barreled up and out.

And into the willing woman beneath me.

I'd promised to pull out that first time. Then things got out of hand. The second and third time, I hadn't said a word.

Maybe it was foolish, but it felt right.

Hell, everything with Tabby felt right.

"Oh God, Tabby... I love you."

I whispered the words again, hoping she would say it back. As usual, she was reserved. For such a fiery, wild looking woman, she was surprisingly restrained. My girl was shy by nature.

Except when I was inside her. My fingers, or tongue or cock.

Then I made her scream like a banshee.

I rested my forehead on hers, not wanting to move out of the circle of her arms. But we had things to do today. Important things.

Getting her a new car was number one.

Moving her the hell out of here was number two.

"Okay lazy bones, time to get up."

She stared up at me, frowning.

"I can't get up if you are on top of me."

I laughed. She had a point there. But she snaked her arms around my neck and smiled shyly.

"Besides, I don't have to be at my 'day job' until nine o'clock."

"Your day job? Is that how you think of me?"

She nodded.

"Yes, it's just a job. Strictly professional."

She squealed as I pinched her ass.

"Well, mostly professional anyway."

I sighed and rolled to the side. We did have to get up. As much as I wanted to stay in bed all day.

"We need to go look at something first anyway."

"What?"

"A car."

"You're getting a new car?"

"No. You are."

"E*xcuse me?"*

I stared at Gabe in shock. He thought he was getting me a car? I didn't have the money for it. He knew that. So that meant...

"You heard me. I can't have you driving around in that piece of junk."

He looked so smug and complacent, lying there in my bed.

"And I want you to move in with me."

"What?"

"I don't like you living over here all by yourself. I want to protect you."

"I don't need your protection- or your charity."

"You do need my protection- and it's not charity. You're mine now. And I'm going to take care of you."

I stood up and started grabbing clothes, not caring if they matched. I just wanted to be covered up. Insulated from his eyes.

From his pity.

"Tabby-"

"You should go. I'll see you later. I need to call the shop."

"That car isn't safe, dammit!"

"It's fine. *I'm fine.*"

He stood up on one leg, totally naked. His thick arm reached out as he braced himself against the wall.

"No, it's not."

"You're crazy. Just because we- it doesn't mean- ugh!"

"Tabby-"

He reached for me but I pulled back.

"I don't need your charity. And I'm not- I'm not going to be providing any other services."

"Tabby-"

"I'm not your live-in sex nurse!"

"I know that! I want you to live with me permanently, dammit! Wherever we end up!"

"Fine!"

He cocked his head, giving me a funny look.

"Did you just agree to move in with me?"

I was breathing heavy. We both were. And the words had just come out. But as soon as they did, I realized I meant them.

"No. But maybe- maybe when we leave."

"We?"

I nodded and his face broke into a wide grin.

"I'll wait to go until you're ready. But I don't think I should work for you anymore."

"Hell, no. That is non-negotiable. And so is the car."

"Gabe-"

"Listen to me Tabby. You are mine and I need to keep you safe. But I'm yours too. So everything I have is yours."

He smiled at me.

"See? I'm really buying myself a car." He pulled me against him and I melted into his big strong chest. Every damn time. I wondered if he would have had that effect on me if I didn't love him. But I did, so it was a moot point.

He brushed my hair away from my face. I sighed as he rubbed his knuckles over my cheek.

"I want you in my house, and in my bed for the rest of your natural born life."

I sighed, shaking my head. His sweet words were making me weak. But I had to maintain my distance. I needed my independence, just in case things went bad.

Otherwise I'd get swept away. I'd be at his mercy. More than I already was.

"No car. But I will come to work. As long as you promise to keep it professional!"

"*While* you are at work." He grinned. "After hours though, you're mine."

I nodded, giving in and he smiled. Gabe pulled me close and kissed me.

And just like that, I had a boyfriend.

GABE

I grinned as I took my pills from my stunning nurse. I was off the pain meds and only on a low-level steroid for inflammation. I was going off those too, dammit. But you had to lower your dose slowly, or all kinds of screwy shit could go down.

I was going to be drug free by the end of the week.

I'd told my doctor I was done and he hadn't fought me on it. Not this time.

I'd told him I was done with the chair too.

I eyed my cane from across the room. Soon. I would be using it soon.

I'd starting rubbing magnesium oil on my leg twice a day. It stung a little but I could tell it was helping. I looked forward to having Tabby help me with a thorough thigh massage.

Top to bottom.

Off-duty of course. Or right before five o'clock. It was safer that way. Because I knew the feeling of her fingers on my thigh would make me hard.

Hell, everything she did made me hard. Always had. The girl just had to breath and I was a drooling animal focused on one thing.

Getting my hands on her.

Speaking of which... Tabby leaned forward and I got a glimpse of her creamy cleavage. She poured me some more freshly squeezed orange juice. Organic too. She'd given my mom a list of stuff she'd learned about in her nutrition class at nursing school.

The two of them were like the food police since I'd come home.

Something about pesticides being full of fluoride, and fluoride pulling calcium from your bones and making muscles and tendons weaker. That was definitely not what I needed at the moment. Or what anyone needed really.

But especially, a two hundred pound guy with thigh muscles that were slowly knitting themselves back together. So I listened, and I let them fuss over me. I appreciated it too.

She was a smart cookie, my Tabby.

Smart *and* delicious.

I resisted the urge to grab her and tug her onto my lap. I could hold her and then tug her top down. Those tits of hers would keep me entertained the rest of the day alone. The rest of her body would take care of at night.

I sighed and let her go about her business instead. She was keeping her promise to stay on as my aid until I was better, and I was doing my best to keep my end of the bargain.

No funny business.

As for the other stuff- well, I hadn't exactly agreed her not to get her a car.

I heard the truck outside and grinned. The fact that Lyle worked at the dealership had definitely made it an easy transaction.

A top of the line, mid-sized SUV, with all the bells and whistles, and at cost. Dark green, to compliment the color of her hazel eyes.

I owed Lyle a solid for this, that was for sure.

I just hoped she liked it.

"Come on, let's go outside."

Tabby gave me a questioning look and I just winked. I shook my head when she held out my jacket. Being around her had me hot and bothered enough.

I could use the cool down to be honest.

She followed me out the sliding doors to the street just as the service center was towing her car away. She ran out and stopped, staring after it. I cringed as the tailpipe fell off, hitting the street with a rattle. Then the truck turned the corner and it was gone.

"Wait- that's my car!"

"Not anymore."

She looked at me, adorably confused. Then understanding dawned. She crossed her arms over her chest and glared at me.

"What did you do, Gabriel?"

Uh oh. She'd never called me by my full name before. I guess it meant I was in trouble.

And I was definitely going to be in trouble for this. But I didn't give a damn. She could glare at me all she wanted. I just wanted her safe.

I grinned at her.

"Took care of my assets."

"Your- assets? Are you implying that I am- an asset?"

"Yes. I am."

Her little mouth opened and closed like a fish. But I had her where I wanted her. The car was on the way to the junkyard where it belonged. The damn thing didn't run anyway.

Now she *had* to take the new car.

I was grinning foolishly when Lyle got out of his car.

"Hey Lyle."

"Looking good, G-man! Now that you are out of that chair, it's time to get wild, right?" Lyle punched my shoulder and smiled sheepishly at Tabby. "Hi Tabby."

She nodded at him, clearly not impressed.

"So here you go, man. The keys to your new ride."

I gestured to Tabby.

"Give them to the lady."

He smiled wide and handed them to Tabby, who took them with a scowl on her face.

"Nice. You guys finally get together?"

I laughed as he wiggled his eyebrows at her.

"He had it bad for you in high school. In case you didn't notice the big guy salivating all over the place every time you were around."

She threw her hands up, but I noticed she was trying not to laugh.

"So he keeps telling me."

"Yeah well, all's well that ends well, right?"

"Whatever you guys say. I'm going inside." She pointed at me. "Do not stay out here in the cold!"

Lyle was grinning as he shouted after her.

"Don't you want to see your new ride?"

She made a dismissive hand gesture and we both laughed. She was sort of a curmudgeon sometimes. But a sexy one. And I liked getting under her skin.

I liked it a lot.

"So, let's grab some beers soon."

I took Lyle's outstretched hand and grinned.

"Sure thing, man. And thanks."

"Anything for love, man. You two... I like it."

I laughed and waved him off. I had to get inside. I knew my woman would be pissed if I stood outside any longer without my jacket.

A few hours later and we'd played gin rummy and five-card stud. I couldn't help playing strip poker in my mind. So far I'd undressed her mentally at least twice. I'd even done two full sets of my PT exercises.

"Uh oh."

Tabby looked up as she shuffled the cards and smiled at me. She was still tiffed about my high-handedness with the car, but I could tell she was pleased too. It would take her a while to get used to me.

She wasn't used to being taken care of. But that was okay. We had plenty of time for her to get used to being my woman. I'd make sure of it.

I grinned at her and scooted closer, taking the cards from her hands.

"Guess what?"

She cocked an eyebrow at me.

"What is it now? A houseboat?"

I let out a bark of laughter. Even when she was cranky, she was the cutest damn thing I'd ever seen. My cute little lady.

"No. It's playtime."

"What?"

I grinned at her and slid my hand up her leg.

"It's after five, sweetheart."

TABBY

I shivered at the promise in his husky voice and smoldering eyes.

Gabe was giving me that look he had. That look that was somehow dark and hot and sweet and hard, all at the same time.

The look that promised I'd be calling out his name before long.

I felt my stomach clench in anticipation, at the same time that I started looking for an escape. There was no way I was going to let him have his way with me with his mother at home. Plus, it was still light outside.

That just wasn't right.

"Come closer."

I looked around, wondering if I should just leave. I could come back late at night. Or just wait for another time.

His lips found my neck before I could decide what to do. I sighed in pleasure as his hot lips found my most sensitive spot. He always seemed to know just where to kiss me... just where to touch me.

I was putty in his hands.

Worse. I was oatmeal.

And Gabe seemed to really have a taste for oatmeal. His hands slid from my waist to my neck where he started unbuttoning my shirt.

"Gabe! Your mother..."

"She won't be home till late."

"Are you sure?"

He murmured yes into my neck, his breath tickling my ear. I gave in with a sigh as his fingers grazed my nipples through my shirt. They were already hard and aching for his touch. I felt a sudden need, deep down in my core.

A need that only Gabe could fill.

I let my head fall back as he pulled my shirt open. He was intent on my breasts as he tugged down my bra cups and moaned like he was in pain. He couldn't seem to get enough of them.

It was crazy to think how wrong I had been. For years I had considered my big breasts to be an embarrassment. Something that just got in the way and made it hard to get to know people or find clothes that fit. In less than a week Gabe had convinced me otherwise.

They were more than a nuisance now. In his hands, they turned into sensitive pleasure domes. For both of us. He loved worshipping them with his lips and hands and tongue. And he couldn't stop looking at me with his hungry eyes. They were open and staring as he devoured me.

I had a feeling he could make me come, just by touching my chest.

My fingers threaded through his hair, marveling at the softness of it. At the realness of his warm head under my hands. This was really happening. We were an item.

This beautiful man loved me.

Gabe Jackson. The same man I'd watched grow up, in the spotlight and in the distance. Somehow, I'd known that we were always aware of each other. Not just as kids growing up in the same town. There was something special between us. I knew where he was without having to think about it, his patterns, his class schedule, his friends.

It was almost like I could sense it when he was near.

Now I knew why.

It's because of *this*. Because we were supposed to do this. Together.

I arched my back as my wonder turned into a climax. I shuddered in ecstasy as he flicked his tongue against my nipple with a satisfied grunt, tweaking the other with his fingertips.

"Ah ah ah!"

My pussy clenched, even without his fingers on me. I felt warmth between my legs and knew I was wet and ready for him. He knew it too. He lifted his head and reached for my jeans, unbuttoning them and pulling them down to my ankles.

"I can't wait."

I nodded breathlessly. I didn't want to wait either. I kicked my boots off and slid out of my jeans as he pulled his pants off. There were crumpled clothes on the floor and two heaving bodies on the couch.

I had a sudden insight: this is what high school romance was *supposed* to be like. Fooling around on the couch. Hiding from your parents. Desperate to be alone together.

Well, at least we were making up for lost time.

We repositioned ourselves on the couch with Gabe on top of me. He exhaled as his bare cock nudged against me, slipping just inside my slick lips.

I moaned in pleasure, at the same time I realized something was missing.

"Gabe?"

He stopped immediately, his face tense as he fought his instincts.

"What about- protection?"

"Shit- Tabby- we haven't been using that lately."

I stared up at him, realizing he was right. That night at my place, he'd asked and I said yes. And we hadn't discussed it again since.

"Oh my God."

"I'm going to do right by you, Tabby. I mean it. I want forever." He grimaced as his cock flexed where he was wedged just inside me. He repeated himself with a groan. "I want forever with you."

I stared at him. Did he mean he wanted to marry me? And have kids? The thought filled me with a sweet longing for little Gabriellas and Gabes running around. I could see them playing in a pretty little yard, with a white picket fence.

And just like that, my heart blossomed. I felt it open and his love poured in, warming me from the inside out. I would have given him anything in that moment. Anything I had to give.

This. I could give him this.

"Do you want me to stop?"

I leaned back and shook my head.

"No."

He held my gaze as he sank inside me. I was keenly aware of his bare cock as he began to move again, his body creating a deliciously slow tempo. He grunted as my body started to undulate in time with his. His hips rotated with purpose, driving up and in, over and over.

We never broke eye contact.

Not as he began to pick up the pace. Not the first time I came. Not the second.

Not when we came together.

Only as he shook with his climax did he look away. And only to pull me close, and bury his face in my hair. I cried out as he thrust into me, harder than ever before. I felt his seed fill me with warm, hot jets.

"God, I love you. I fucking love you Tabby!"

I held him tightly as our bodies trembled with the force of our release. He loved me. Even if it was partly just the crazy pull we had towards each other, I knew he meant it. I could feel it in my bones.

I could not stop smiling as we lay there, tangled up on the sofa. I was still smiling when he kissed me and pulled away. We dressed slowly, his eyes focused on my curves. I still felt shy at the way he stared at my body, but it made me proud too.

He wanted *me.*

Shabby Tabby.

Well, I didn't feel like that same girl anymore. I felt like a woman. I felt like *his* woman.

We watched TV on the couch for a while, then I whipped up a quick dinner of reheated organic chicken breast with a chilled quinoa and zucchini salad.

Gabe pulled me up against his side as we ate. He squeeze me and fed me bites off his plate. Then we finished mine.

It was like he had to be touching me at all times. To make sure I was real. That I was his.

I had to admit, I knew the feeling. I was afraid to close my eyes. Afraid he would disappear.

It was around nine when his mom came in. I got up to put on my coat.

"Don't go."

I shook my head.

"I have to."

"At least wait untill mom comes down. I want to tell her about us."

I paused, my hand on my coat zipper. He looked so earnest. So sincere. But this was happening too fast. I shook my head.

"Not tonight. Soon. Okay?"

GABE

I caught her hand before she could leave.

"I have to go. I have some of Gran's stuff to ship."

I stared at her blankly. I didn't want Tabby to go. But I also knew she wasn't going to necessarily let me make love to her again either.

Not until she was sure my mom was asleep anyway.

An ugly suspicion started to form in my mind. Did she have a place to go already? Had she made plans to return to school? I didn't know what she was thinking and I hated it.

"Ship where?"

"Different places. Mostly Brooklyn and LA. I'm selling it all online. Some of it's collectible. Or the hipsters seem to think so anyway."

She smiled at me softly.

"Who knew Gran had such good taste."

I let my breath out in a whoosh. She was just selling stuff. She wasn't leaving town yet.

She wasn't leaving me.

"Okay. What about tomorrow night? Can we go to your place?"

She shrugged gracefully. I wanted to pull her back into my lap. I didn't want to wait until tomorrow, dammit!

"I have to work the late shift."

"Okay, I'll come to you. Lyle wants to have drinks anyway."

She smiled at me shyly and pressed a quick kiss to my lips. I grabbed her and pulled her close while I ravaged her mouth with my tongue. We were both out of breath when she lifted her head again.

"Are you sure you won't stay?" I wiggled my eyebrows. "We could be real quiet."

She laughed and shook her head. At the doorway she turned back and dangled the keys in the air.

"Good night Gabe. And... thanks."

I nodded and watched her leave. Even with that big old coat of hers, she looked like a fashion model. I wondered how she would look in fancy girly stuff. Or pink.

Or red.

I realized I was getting hard again, just thinking about her dressed up in something pretty. I was going to take her shopping I decided. Or just pick out some stuff online.

Maybe some lingerie too.

I pulled out my laptop and started picking stuff out at one of the big department stores. I started with intimates. The lacier the better. Pink, white, red. Silks and satins. Stuff to sleep in and stuff *not* to sleep in.

I realized I was doing everything backwards and only worrying about what I would like. For a minute, I imagined her slapping my face instead of falling into my bed.

But hell, she didn't have to know that I'd started with the naughty stuff. I looked at coats next, thinking she needed something warm and waterproof.

Then I got her a hat, scarf and gloves to match, all in cashmere. Then a couple of sweaters and jeans and tops. Sexy slinky tops. Stuff that would cling to her curves, not hide them.

I picked out some more, realizing I was going overboard and not caring. I got her a couple of dresses and some skirts. I had fun picking out some high heels, as well as a pair of cute little boots and some kicks. I was about to check out when I decided to get her a purse.

And panties. Lots of sexy little panties.

Tabby might get annoyed that I wanted to dress her up. She'd probably say I was controlling.

And she'd be right.

Not that I'd ever wanted to control a woman before. But with her it was different. I wanted to keep her close and keep her safe. I wanted everything to be better for her.

I wanted to dress her, and undress her. Mostly the latter. I closed my eyes and pictured her trying on all the clothes and then letting me tear them off of her again.

Damn, that was gonna be hot!

I was getting hard so I checked out and took a cold shower. It barely made a dent in my boner, but it was better than nothing. I knew my mom would be down soon and that just wasn't right.

She popped her head down when she heard me coming out of the bathroom. The walker might help me get around easier, but that thing was loud.

"Hey."

"Hey mom. Come down. I want to talk to you."

"What's up?"

"It's about Tabby."

She sat down and handed me a glass of juice to take my night pills with.

"Oh yeah? Did she finally agree to go out with you then?"

I stared at my mom in shock. How the hell did she know? Then I started laughing.

"Am I that obvious?"

She cocked an eyebrow at me.

"Son, you might as well have been wearing a sign."

I shook my head, realizing she knew me better than I knew myself.

"Did you know when you hired her?"

She shrugged. "I had a feeling. But I wasn't matchmaking if that's what you are asking."

"Well, you did a better job than you know." I smiled at my mother. "Because I'm going to marry her."

My mom looked shocked for half a second. And then she smiled bigger than I'd ever seen in my life.

"Does she know that?"

I smiled back.

"Not yet. But she will real soon."

She clicked her tongue at me.

"Good luck son. I think you might need it."

TABBY

"Can I get you anything else?"

"How about your phone number?"

I rolled my eyes at the middle-aged guy staring at me with unconcealed lust. The idiot was married too. Gross.

I looked up and saw Gabe was sitting at the bar, watching me like a hawk. It made it a lot easier to handle this sort of thing without getting too upset.

Plus, I didn't want him pummeling the customers.

"Anything *on* the menu."

"Damn girl, that's cold."

The guy didn't seem too embarrassed about being turned down in front of his friends. His buddy elbowed him and leered at my chest. I ignored them and set the check down on the table.

"Okay, here's your check. Come again."

"We sure will sweet thing."

I shook my head and left, making my rounds through the restaurant. I did my best to be polite, even when the customers weren't. I didn't even care about tips when things got like that.

I just wanted to keep my job.

So I had to resist the urge to dump a drink down their pants.

Gabe was watching me. I could feel his eyes on me. He smiled at me warmly and I blushed. Suddenly, things didn't seem all that bad.

The rest of the night passed in a blur. I knew when I got off Gabe was coming home with me.

And I knew he was going to keep me up all night.

I definitely didn't mind though.

Like clockwork, round eleven the rowdy crowd came in. I watched as Gabe was surrounded by his old teammates. He even did some shots with them.

I left him alone, bringing him a snack at one point but letting him have his fun. It's not like he was still on pain killers or anything.

It was getting near closing when things got weird. The place was emptying out, with last call over and done with. Gabe's friends had just left as I headed to the back.

I turned the corner and froze.

Gabe was staring at me with a strange look in his eyes. He leaned in the hallway, his walker blocking my path.

"Almost ready?"

I nodded breathlessly, wondering what he had in mind. He'd blindfolded me the other night. I shivered just thinking about it.

The truth was though, I liked to see his beautiful face when he took me.

I especially liked to watch him as he watched *us*.

"Let me get my things."

He didn't say a word, just stared at me. His face was strange- almost hard. I felt a tiny pinprick of worry. A feeling that something was off. But it was just Gabe. He loved me.

Nothing was wrong.

Nothing could be.

I gathered my things and said goodnight to the other girls. Gabe was waiting outside by my car. He stared at it, barely looking at me when I unlocked the door for him.

We drove across town without talking. Every time I glanced at him, he was staring out the window in silence. He didn't try and take my hand. He didn't try and kiss me.

He didn't say a single word.

I swallowed, feeling suddenly nervous. Maybe something *was* wrong. Maybe he was regretting getting me the car.

Or asking me to move in with him.

Or any of it.

I decided I should tell him he didn't need to do anything for me. That it wouldn't change a thing about how I felt about him.

I wanted to tell him, but I couldn't work up the courage to say anything. And he didn't say a word. Not until we got all the way inside. He locked the door and turned to face me.

"Take your clothes off."

My mouth opened a little. I realized I was nervous but pushed the feeling aside. We'd already done this a bunch of times. He loved me. That's what mattered. He was just eager to make love.

What was there to be nervous about?

I smiled at him shyly. "Do you want to go into the bedroom?" He just stared at me, his jaw clenched.

"No need."

"Okay."

I watched him sit on the couch and push the walker away. Then he unbuttoned his jeans and leaned back. He didn't even take his coat off. He just stared at me, waiting.

I fidgeted a little. My gut was telling me something was wrong. I just didn't know what it was.

"Is everything okay?"

"Why wouldn't it be?"

He looked straight at me, almost challenging me to say something. I felt flustered, like I was trying to prove something. I just didn't know *what.*

"You're just- you're being..."

"What am I being?"

Gabe's face was calm. He didn't look mad. He raised his eyebrows and I forced myself to answer him.

"Different, I guess."

He shrugged, completely indifferent. I would have thought we were strangers, except I could see the fire in his eyes and the growing bulge in his pants. Maybe he didn't feel like talking.

That was it, right?

"What are you waiting for?"

I bit my lip and started pulling my clothes off. My jacket. My scarf. My t-shirt.

"That's good. Keep going."

I stared at him, standing there in my bra and jeans. This felt weird. Wrong somehow.

Like we weren't together. Like I was just- an object.

Like I was a stripper or something.

"You can have the car back."

He stared at me, a muscle ticking in his jaw.

"Keep it. I want you to have it."

"I'm just saying if that's what's bothering you-"

He sighed, like he was bored. But he undid his pants and shrugged out of his jacket. Then he leaned back and looked at me again.

"The car is yours. Now take your bra off."

I reached for the clasp and undid it. But I didn't pull it off my shoulders. Instead, I covered myself with my hands.

Suddenly, I was on the verge of tears.

"Come here, Tabby."

"Are you angry with me?"

"Come here and make it up to me."

"Make... what up?"

He smiled at me coldly.

"Come here and I'll tell you."

GABE

I couldn't stop hearing the words. The sick, twisted words that were ripping and shredding my heart.

'Had her the other night. Love that little mole on the back of her neck. She has a matching one right above her sweet ass.'

The guy talking was an idiot. I never would have given it a second thought. Except, Tabby *did* have a mole on her neck. And one on her lower back.

And Pete's buddy Josh had known that.

How the fuck had he known?

And where the fuck was she going on the nights she wasn't with me?

Apparently, I was being made a fool of. She was cheating on me, and not even being discreet about it.

There was absolutely no way for Josh to know any of that. Unless he'd seen it himself.

Tabby was playing me. And playing me hard.

But that didn't mean I didn't want her. I did. I wanted her to tell me the truth. The truth. That was a laugh.

I probably wouldn't believe a word that came out of her sweet lying little mouth. But first I wanted her to give me what she'd given him. I wanted a pound of flesh, and then some.

I wanted to ride.

All that time I'd been gentle. All that time I'd waited for my chance... I'd been an idiot. Even if she had been a virgin, which I was starting to doubt, she'd definitely been with someone else since.

At least one someone, if not more.

She was a fast worker. And tonight she was going to make it up to me.

Or at least start to try.

She looked so nervous, standing there, with her hands over her gorgeous tits. That perfect body, that I'd thought was all mine. Well, it wasn't.

All the rumors. They'd been true. And I was too stupid to see it.

I never would have believed it but I had proof. The moles. The things he'd said about her riding him all night.

It was all true.

Well, fuck it. I might not trust her anymore, but I was nowhere near satisfied. I still wanted her, more than I cared to admit. If she knew tricks, I wanted to see them all.

"I said, come here."

And she did. She looked so sweet and nervous, that if I hadn't heard what those guys had said- I would have folded her into my arms and told her she was beautiful. That she had nothing to be shy about. That she drove me crazy.

That I loved her.

Love.

What a joke. I was just the dumbest guy in a town full of guys who'd put their mark on Tabby, way before me.

I reached for her jeans, tugging them down her hips. She stepped out of them and I guided her onto my lap. I wanted to fuck her out of my system, though I doubted I could do that in one night.

I had to get her on the regular for a couple of months at least. But I'd have to make sure she didn't fuck around on me.

I pulled her panties to the side and stared down at her perfect little pussy. She must have been born with superior genes.

I spit on my hand and rubbed my fingers against her. She sighed as I played with her pussy lips, pressing just inside. She was so small and tight and already getting wet for me. I couldn't wait to get inside her.

My cock jumped and I pulled it out, pressing it against her lips. Then I gripped her juicy hips and pressed her down on me. She gasped as I pushed her lower and lower until she was impaled.

I held her down on me, waiting for her body to open. Usually, I'd have waited till she was more ready. But I didn't feel like waiting tonight.

She felt so fucking good. So perfect and sweet and good. I closed my eyes, wanting to pretend she was the same girl I'd held just a day before.

But she wasn't.

"Take your bra off."

I licked my lips as she slid the plain white bra off her shoulders. She didn't dress like a tramp, or even a girl with a boyfriend, let alone many. I wouldn't let that distract me from the truth though.

Or my own pleasure.

I pulled her forward so that her breasts were hanging in front of my face like ripe fruit. I licked one and then the other as I started to fuck her from beneath. I grunted as her tightness pulled me in further, sucking at me like quicksand.

That's what she was. Dangerous quicksand. She seemed so solid- so real- but take one wrong step and boom- you were done for.

Well, I knew now. So I could take what I wanted and that was it. I wasn't going to drown or get buried alive.

I was just going to get off and desperately try to get her out of my system.

She started circling her hips on mine. She definitely knew what the hell she was doing. It was so hot, watching her work herself on my shaft as her perfect body jiggled in front of my eyes.

I knew I could come soon. I didn't hold back, driving up and into her again and again. At the last minute I pulled out, spraying her belly with my seed.

"Oh!"

She looked surprised as hell, and still horny. Good. I wasn't even close to being finished with her.

"Get yourself cleaned up."

I wouldn't need long before round two. I leaned back and waited for her to come back so we could go again.

She brought me a glass of water, taking a sip after I did. She set it down and let me guide her onto her back. I pulled the rest of my clothes off and climbed on top of her.

She took a deep breath and raised her eyes to me.

"I love you."

I pushed my bare cock inside her with a groan.

And said nothing.

TABBY

I slid my arms around Gabe's neck, clinging to him as he rode me. He wasn't being gentle like usual but I didn't mind. As long as he held me in his strong arms, I didn't mind anything.

"Fuck, you feel so good. How could you feel so good?"

He grunted and I felt him twitch inside me. I was close to coming, even though something felt weird. Then I figured out what it was.

He wasn't kissing me. Not once. Or telling me I was beautiful. He was barely touching me.

He was just... fucking.

"That's it baby. Come for me."

And I did.

He rode through my orgasm, his sexy groans making me come even harder.

"You like that, don't you?"

I whimpered as he tweaked my nipple.

"Why Tabby? Fuck. Fuck, why pretend? We could have been doing this all along."

I was in a post orgasmic haze but I opened my eyes, forcing myself to look at him. He was fucking me faster now. Harder.

He cursed and I felt him come inside me. I squeezed his shoulders as he shuddered helplessly. He opened his eyes and stared down at me. His eyes were confused.

I realized what had been bothering me.

It was the first emotion he'd shown all night.

"You still make me feel like no one else."

Still? What was he talking about? He didn't pull out. I felt him getting hard again inside me. He moaned and squeezed my breast. Then he started to move.

"How many others have there been? How many this week?"

"What?"

He reached down to play with my body, his fingers on my clit.

"Just tell me. There's no reason to lie anymore. I told you you could keep the car."

"Ah!"

I came again as he strummed my clit faster and faster. But something was wrong- something-

"I don't even care if you fuck them in it. I just want you to be safe."

I was still coming but alarm bells were going off. What was he talking about? Gabe exhaled heavily as he lowered his lips to my breasts.

"Even now I can't resist you. Or this body."

"Wait-"

He growled as he flicked his tongue over my nipples, driving into me. He stared up at me, his eyes blazing.

"You must think I'm an idiot."

Then he came. He lay on top of me, breathing heavily. When he lifted his head he gave me a cold look.

"Gabe?"

"Want to go for round four? I don't have anyplace better to be."

"No." I knew now. I knew that he had changed his mind. I pushed at his shoulders. "Get off of me."

He pulled out with a grunt.

"Jesus, how could you feel so good?"

I bit back a cry. He was talking to me like I was a tramp. Like he'd thought that all along.

"Stop talking to me like that."

He shrugged and pulled his jeans on.

"Like what? Like you've been doing half the guys in this town and lying to me about it?"

I stared at him, my mouth open. My voice was thin, reedy. Like a little girl begging for scraps.

For kindness.

"You're just drunk Gabe. You should go home."

"Yeah, I'm drunk. It doesn't mean you haven't been playing me."

"I was a virgin. You know I didn't-"

He grabbed my arm, forcing me to look at him.

"Don't lie to me."

"I'm not!"

He reached out to stroke my face.

"I don't care. I still want you. If you stop seeing the rest of them, we can see how this goes."

He laughed, the sound harsh and bitter.

"How crazy is that? I don't even care. I will keep you too busy to fuck anyone else."

I started crying then. He frowned and reached for me.

"Don't cry, Tabby. I said I would give you another chance. I just wish you hadn't lied."

I pushed his hands away and grabbed my shirt, holding it in front of me. I didn't want him looking at me anymore.

I didn't want him to see me.

"Get out."

He stared at me, his jaw ticking. I scrambled for my purse and chucked the keys at him.

"Take your fucking car keys."

He put his boots on, talking the whole time.

"I didn't ask for any of this, you know. You show up, looking like a lost puppy. I didn't ask to be fucking lied to!"

Very slowly, he stood up and put the rest of his clothes on. He dropped the keys on the floor with a thud.

"Keep the fucking car. You earned it."

And then he was gone.

I stood there in the living room naked, wrapped in a baggy t-shirt while the cold air blew into the house. I forced myself to move, to shut the door. To feed the cat.

To take a shower.

No matter what I did though, I couldn't wash his touch away. I couldn't wash away his words.

Or the cold look in his eyes.

I crawled into bed and cried myself to sleep.

GABE

I stared out at the snow that was falling. It was pretty.

A picturesque view of our beautiful, postcard seaside town.

I wanted to smash something.

I hadn't slept at all. Instead I'd pulled out a bottle of whiskey and started in on it, steadily working my way towards the bottom.

It was nearly empty, but not quite.

"Is Tabby coming today?"

My mom's head appeared at the top of the stairs.

"No. I don't need an aid anymore."

"You sure?"

I nodded and pushed the bottle under the couch. Mom didn't need to see that. I'd throw it out later.

And find a way to get a new one. I planned to be drunk as much as possible going forward. Until I could erase the feel of Tabby's skin underneath my hands. Her body underneath me.

The look of pain and betrayal in her eyes.

I cursed myself and swigged the last sip of booze. Then I picked up my phone and texted Lyle. If I was going to spend the day drinking, I might as well have company.

Plus, I needed someone to bring me more booze.

I leaned back and closed my eyes, seeing the look of hurt and confusion on her beautiful face. She'd seemed so sincere. She'd even told me she loved me.

After all the times I'd had to drag it out of her, now she tells me.

Now that I knew her for what she really was.

I rubbed my face, trying to rub the thoughts away. I'd been so close to proposing. I'd even looked at rings.

We could have been so happy together. But I would have been married to a lie.

I decided I didn't care. I would let her move in with me anyway. I still felt protective of her.

I would keep her under lock and key. Then maybe if she proved herself to me, I would reconsider marrying her after all.

Because despite it all, I was still in love with her.

I heard my mom locking the front door and pulled the bottle back out.

It was going to be a long day.

TABBY

I stared at the ceiling for twenty minutes before I got out of bed. I knew I wasn't going in to work today.

I was never going back there again.

I forced myself to call the service and let them know I wasn't going back. I didn't offer any explanation and they didn't ask. At this point, I wasn't asking for references anyway.

I'd be long gone, as soon as I could figure out where I was going.

Far, far away from here.

As far from Gabe Jackson as humanly possible. I thought if I ever saw him again, I'd shatter into a million pieces. And there would be no putting me back together again.

I'd been tempted, so pathetically tempted, to take him up on the scraps he was offering. That he'd 'take me back' if I behaved myself.

No mention of love. No talk of the future. All of that was gone- but why? Because something had finally convinced him that the rumors about me had been true all along.

A knock on the door had my heart pounding. I realized I was wearing one of Gabe's shirts and yanked it off. I must have put it on in the middle of the night.

Yeah, I was that pitiful. But I still had my pride.

If he was back- if he saw me wearing his shirt- I couldn't bear it.

I pulled on a dressing robe and opened the door. No one was there. But I'd gotten a delivery.

Boxes and boxes. And all of them said Bloomingdales.

I frowned, thinking there must be a mistake. I'd never ordered anything that fancy before in my life. I checked the name on the shipping label and sure enough, it was mine.

All eight of them.

I dragged the boxes inside and opened one. I knew I would have to send it back. Maybe it was a prank or- my breath caught in my throat when I saw the note attached to the receipt, with all the prices crossed out.

Only the best for my girl. Love, Gabe.

And that was it. The slim shred of control I had left just snapped. I slid to the floor, unable to stop the tears from falling.

I didn't know what I had done to have lost his love, but I knew it was gone.

He *had* loved me. I knew it.

And now, he didn't.

I wasn't going to let it destroy me, dammit. I could feel the will to leave town slipping away. I could feel the urge to go to him, to beg his forgiveness for something I had never done.

To beg him to love me again. But that wasn't how love worked.

To hell with that.

I loved Gabe. I didn't know if I would ever stop loving him. But this was bullshit. He was being an ass, and for no good reason.

If being loved by him had taught me one thing, it was that I deserved better than this.

And I was going to get it. No matter how long it took, I would find a way to stand on my own two feet and know that I deserved to be loved again.

Even if I never got over him, I would not be second best, or something he 'learned to live with.'

He could take his 'forgiveness' and shove it up his ass.

I pulled the envelope of tips out from under my mattress and started counting. I had a couple thousand bucks. Plus, a few more in the bank.

I spent the next few hours cleaning and boxing the last of Grandma's trinkets. Maybe I'd just take it all with me, deal with selling it wherever I landed.

I didn't need to stay here after all.

I could work a few more shifts and-

No. I sat down hard again. Gabe could come in. He probably would. And he'd make me the same callous offer, and I'd find it hard to say no.

I didn't think I could bear to face him. Not for a minute. Or any of his buddies.

Once his friends knew we weren't together anymore, they'd be even worse than usual. I'd be fair game again.

Or worse, I'd have to see him with someone else. If I was fair game, so was he. Right? He could just move on and get a new girlfriend. Or two.

Even though I knew what a cruel bastard he could be, he was still a catch. Any girl would bend over backwards to be with him.

Just like I had.

No. I would just leave. I'd been planning to go in six weeks anyway. I'd just move up my exit date and put in my notice.

I called the U-Haul place and my friends. I didn't go into details but I did tell Jacks that things had gone spectacularly wrong.

Dennis invited me down to Florida. Maryann invited me to Denver. Jackie invited me to Paris.

Well, I couldn't take the damn cat to Paris with me.

I decided to get a truck and hit the road. I could check out a couple spots on the way to see my friends. And then maybe when I found a place, I could start saving up money for school again.

Maybe I could even begin to heal my heart.

But none of that was going to happen if I didn't start prepping. I loaded Gabe's car with stuff for the thrift store and got to work.

GABE

ou look like shit, man."

I grunted and handed Lyle a hundred dollar bill for the booze I'd asked for. A whole fucking case of it. He waved me off but I insisted.

I wanted to get mind numbingly drunk with a clear conscious.

Well, mostly clear.

I couldn't shake the look of hurt in Tabby's eyes. The sound of her voice as she'd told me she loved me... and when she'd told me to get out. She'd looked absolutely crushed when I left her place.

Crushed and innocent. And so damn beautiful it hurt to think about it.

Remember Gabe. Remember the betrayal.

What a deceptive little liar she was. Everything about her was a sham. Except her looks. Those were natural. And the kindness she'd shown me. Even if she was just doing her job.

And her loneliness.

Shit, I was talking myself back into loving her again, not that I'd really stopped. But I knew I couldn't trust her. I cursed and grabbed a bottle. I couldn't open it fast enough.

"It's a little early isn't it?"

"It's five o'clock somewhere."

He laughed and shrugged, pouring himself a drink too. He talked and I listened, not saying much. Not until he mentioned the 'T' word.

"How's Tabby liking the car?"

I shrugged. I did not have a clue what to say. I'm sure Lyle was in on the joke along with everyone else. I didn't blame him for not telling me. He probably didn't realize how far deep I was.

"We split up but I told her to keep it."

He raised his eyebrows and sipped his drink. I was already refilling my glass.

"That's an expensive parting gift."

"Small price to pay for escaping matrimony."

"Matrimony? No shit!"

"Yeah well, I wised up before it got to that point. Apparently I'm the only guy in town who didn't get a taste."

He gave me an odd look.

"That old shit? I don't believe it."

I stared at him.

"You don't believe what?"

"Pete and his crew. They are always making up stories about this girl or that one. They act like they've fucked the whole damn town."

"Yeah, well they weren't making this up."

"How do you know?"

I looked at him. I looked at the bottle. I poured another drink.

"Pete's friend knew about things. Things you would have had to be there to know."

"There-there?"

"Yeah."

I drank.

"Oof. That's rough, man. I always thought she got a bad rap. This town is so boring people latch on to anything."

"I thought you liked it here."

"It's okay. I think about leaving sometimes, like you did. But my old man needs me."

I drank. He drank. It was a while before anyone talked again. Thankfully, the world was starting to get nice and blurry around the edges.

"What did he know, if you don't mind my asking?"

"He knew about her… body."

"Like what man? Or is it too personal?"

I laughed bitterly. Everyone in the whole fucking town knew more about her than me.

"No man, it's nothing gross. He just knew about her beauty marks."

"What the hell is a beauty mark?"

I snorted and took a deep pull. It didn't even burn anymore. That's when you knew you were on the short road to an epic drunk.

"It's a mole. Mole, beauty mark, same thing. That's what my mom calls them. I must be fuckin' drunk."

I laughed again but Lyle looked thoughtful.

"You're going to kill me man but I swear to God I know something about that."

"What?"

"We were one year ahead of her right? And Topher?"

"Yeah? So?"

"Let me call him, see if I'm right."

He went outside to make a call. I finished my drink and poured another one. I was so fucking miserable I didn't think I could stand it. I was getting plastered and it was barely early afternoon.

And it still wasn't enough.

But if I could blot her out, it was worth it. Besides, its not like I had anywhere to be.

"He's coming over after his shift. I told him to bring beer and pizza."

"And more whiskey."

Lyle shook his head.

"Whatever you want man. You're the war hero."

I snorted.

"It was a fucking valve malfunction. I didn't do shit."

"You shoved some guy out of the way didn't you?"

I stared at him.

"Yeah."

He poured us each another drink and toasted me.

"So, you're a fucking hero. Deal with it."

TABBY

I stared at the two sets of keys in my hand. I had done everything even faster than I'd imagined. The thought of staying in this town one more second had lit a fire under my butt.

I was ready.

And I didn't need Gabe's pity-mobile anymore.

I swallowed and stuck the keys in an envelope. I could have kept the car and paid him back eventually. But that didn't sit right.

Besides, I didn't want anything to remind me of him. I knew I'd be thinking about him anyway. Why make things worse?

He had burned a hole in my soul. He had opened my eyes and my heart to love. And then he'd smashed it.

I still didn't understand why, but it didn't matter.

It was time to move on. I couldn't stop myself from crying, but I wasn't going to let anyone around here see me do it either.

Especially not Gabe.

I stuck the envelope in the mailbox and shut the door. That was that. He'd get the keys in a few days. And I'd be long gone.

I hoped Lyle could take the car back. It was still new. Maybe they'd consider it an extra long test drive.

I slid my hands against each other. There, that was done. Now all I had to do was finish loading the van and say goodbye to Shortie.

I felt bad about that. I'd quit abruptly but he wasn't mad. He'd always had a soft spot for me.

I guess that sort of thing happened a lot in the food service industry anyway.

Either that, or he'd heard the absolute misery in my voice when I called in. I might be able to hide my tears, but the rest of me was clearly heartbroken.

The handoff was pretty easy. I drove through town and pulled in to the back of Garrity's. I'd brought my apron and he'd brought me my last check.

Then we hugged and said goodbye.

I climbed into the van and locked my seatbelt into place. A loud mewling made me roll my eyes.

"Oh shut up. I'd be on a plane to Paris if it weren't for you."

But I smiled a little. At least I had Petunia for company. Right now it was just the two of us against the world.

I drove to the edge of town, not glancing right or left. No need for last looks. I had enough bad memories to last me a lifetime.

I pulled onto the highway and never looked back.

GABE

"Toph! Toph! Toph! Toph!"

I opened a bleary eye as Lyle chanted and pumped his fist into the air. Topher took one look at the two of us and laughed.

"Jesus, what the hell have the two of you been up to down here?"

"Glory days, man. Relivin' the glory days."

I moaned, rubbing my head. I felt like shit. And not just from the booze. A few days ago I'd had it all figured out. I'd had the girl of my dreams on lockdown.

Now, I was drunk in a rec room with two dudes.

And she was… well, God knows where she was. Or who she was with. I'd basically told her I'd give her a second chance if she stopped seeing other guys.

I knew it was stupid, but I couldn't help it. Even with all her lies, I wanted her.

"Gabe got dumped. He's commiserating. No-convalescing!"

"Dumped? I didn't know you had a lady."

"Tabitha Peterson."

"No shit? That was a long time coming. That's why you wanted this?"

He held up a yearbook in one hand and a twelve-pack of beer in the other. Then he jerked his head over his shoulder.

"Pizza's on its way."

"You rock, man. Sit down. Try not to make the G-Man dizzy."

Topher sat and placed the yearbook on the table. I squinted at it, accepting a cold beer and twisting the top off.

"What is that?"

"You wanted this right? That picture of her? Heads rolled over this one, let me tell you. I think the yearbook editor lost his scholarship for sticking that picture in there."

"What the fuck are you talking about?"

He laughed.

"That sexy ass mole. Man, that thing went down in history at Heckam High let me tell you."

"Mole?"

"Yeah. Here, let me show you-" He picked up the yearbook and started flipping through it. Towards the back were the candid shots of seniors. He held up the book and grinned at me.

There was a huge picture of Tabby and a couple other girls. She was sitting on the bleachers, staring over her shoulder with a look of annoyance.

She looked so young and sweet. Absolutely stunning as usual. But that's not what caught my attention. No, it was her clearly visible lower back. Someone had lifted her shirt to snap her bra at the exact second the picture was taken.

The shot was sexy as hell. She looked like a pin up girl, surprised as a puppy tugged her bikini strap down. Except she'd just been a girl minding her own business and someone had bothered her.

I felt sick as I stared at the photo.

Her entire lower back was exposed, right down to the dimples above her ass. You could see the graceful line of her spine, the side of her breasts, and yes, the famous mole.

She was wearing a pony tail. So you could see the mole on her neck, too.

"This photo was ripped out of every guy's yearbook when they went off to college, let me tell you."

"Not yours Toph?" Lyle was cackling and sipping a beer. Meanwhile, I felt like I was cracking in two.

Toph shrugged.

"No man, I'm a gentleman. Besides, I didn't go to college!"

My heart slammed in my chest.

I was an idiot. I was a fucking idiot. The biggest fucking idiot on the whole damn planet.

She hadn't fucked that cretin. She hadn't fucked anyone. She hadn't done a damn thing except be the sweetest, most loving girl I'd ever met.

And I'd treated her like shit.

Like worse than shit. Like she was a thing- an object to be used for pleasure. An object that I hadn't wanted anyone else getting their hands on.

I closed my eyes, seeing her lying beneath me. Hearing her tell me she loved me. And I had just… used her to get off.

"Oh fuck."

"You okay G-man?"

"No. I'm not fucking okay."

I grabbed my phone and called her. No answer. I texted her.

Where are you

I need to talk
I'm an idiot

No response. Not that I was surprised. I was sure she hated me.

Hell, *I* hated me.

"Pizza's here!"

I dragged my wallet out and paid the guy. Then I whispered in a ragged voice.

"Coffee. Water. Gatorade."

"You want to sober up man?"

I nodded and Lyle slapped my back.

"Alright man, we got you. Why don't you start with a shower?"

I was careful as I used the walker to get into the bathroom. I was almost ready to graduate to the cane but now was not the time.

My mind was racing as I tried to figure out what to do. I needed to go find Tabby but I was in no condition. If she saw me like this, she wouldn't even give me the time of day.

Not that I blamed her.

But I did need to find her. Start the ball rolling. I had to make things right. I stared at my bleary eyes in the mirror.

I had to fix this.

I leaned my head out of the bathroom as the steam started to fill the room.

"You okay?"

"Call Garrity's. Find out if she's working tonight."

When I came out, Lyle was brewing coffee at the breakfast bar. Topher was eating a slice and flipping through his old yearbook. Actually, they'd found mine somewhere too.

"Holy shit, were we ever this young?"

I shook my head and took a slice. If I ate, I might sober up faster. I might be able to think straight.

"Hey man."

"I need to get into town. I need to see her. Is anyone sober enough to drive?"

They exchanged a look and I put my pizza down. I knew it was something bad without even having to ask.

"What is it?"

"I called the bar, man. They said she.." Lyle's voice drifted off and I started imagining all sorts of things. She refused to come to the phone. She had a restraining order. She had a new boyfriend already.

"She what?"

"She quit man. They said she, uh, she left town. She's gone."

The walls came crashing in on me. She was gone. She'd really left. That innocent, beautiful girl was out there alone somewhere, with no one to help her or protect her.

And it was all my fucking fault.

I thought I'd hit bottom ten minutes ago when I realized what an idiot I was. An idiot and a cold-hearted bastard who had mistreated the most important person in the world to me.

But I hadn't believed for an instant that I'd truly lost her.

Not until now.

TABBY

I drove all night. The pain wouldn't let me stop. My pride wouldn't either.

It was safer this way.

I had to get far away so that I wouldn't go crawling back. Wouldn't demean myself by taking what scraps Gabe offered me. Wouldn't let him have me without loving me.

Because even now, I was tempted to.

The things he could do to me with his body… the way he made me feel. There was nothing like it. The pleasure had eclipsed all my doubts and opened my heart.

I wanted it still. I craved it.

Even though it had almost destroyed me.

I fought back tears, realizing I could still feel him inside me. It was already a few days and it was like it had just happened. It was so fresh.

It was around dawn when I crossed the state line into Maryland. My eyes were blurry and my head hurt. Even my hands were tired from gripping the wheel.

But as I watched the sun come up over the bay, I let myself relax. I was far enough now. I had severed every single thing that connected me to home.

I never had to go back. I had no reason to go back now.

I winced, my thoughts immediately on Gabe. Missing him. Wondering how he was. If he was taking his vitamins. Doing his exercises.

If he was overdoing it.

Or if he was with someone else yet.

It wasn't my problem now. I mentally wished him the best in his recovery and tried to shut the door on any thoughts of him. But as I sat there in the rental truck, parked in a rest stop, I couldn't help but wonder how things had come to this.

I had resisted checking my phone, knowing I would be crushed if he hadn't called me. Or, even worse, if he had spewed more of his cruel accusations.

So I hadn't looked at it at all. Which was a good thing, since I'd been focused on the road instead.

I exhaled and reached into my bag, slowly pulling out my phone. It was on silent, for safer driving. I didn't need to be distracted.

Plus, the only people on Earth who cared about me anymore all knew I was on the road. I smiled ruefully. Thank goodness for friends and social misfits.

But my phone wasn't blank. I had missed calls and messages. Lots and lots of messages. All from Gabe.

Well, shit.

My heart thudded in my chest as I flipped through them, chewing on my lip. Gabe was demanding to see me. He said he needed to talk to me. His messages got increasingly aggressive and desperate sounding.

He didn't seem mad at me anymore though. He seemed upset. I stared at the phone, reading the messages over and over again.

Where are you
I need to talk
I'm an idiot

Then an hour after that:

Please baby. Let me know you are alright. Let me know you don't hate me.

Then another hour later there was more:

I'm going out of my head Tabby. I got so jealous, I didn't think. I swear to you it will never happen again.

And then just a few minutes ago:

Dammit Tabby get your ass back here! Where the hell are you? You cant just go running off because we had a fight!

I gripped the phone tightly. A fight? He called accusing me of cheating on him a fight?

I pecked out a response, too angry to give a damn.

You have a lot of nerve Gabe Jackson. Go to hell.

I resisted the urge to tell him to take his medicine. It was hard, but I held back. I was proud of myself. He wrote back immediately. Jeez, it was six am. He must have been staring at his phone.

Where are you. Come home now.

No. You can't tell me what to do.

Yes I can! You're my girlfriend dammit! You can't just leave town!

I'm not your girlfriend, remember?

Yes you fucking are.

You wanted me to prove to you that I could be trusted.

I didn't mean it Tabby. Please come back. I'm an idiot.
I love you.

No. I can't. I can't be with someone who thinks that I'm- well, you know what you thought.

I chewed my lip for a minute and then gave in to temptation.

Take care of yourself. And take your medicine!
Goodbye.

Then I quickly turned my phone off before I could cave in. Gabe was confusing me. He kept saying sweet things mixed in with all the stupid things.

Like that I was still his girlfriend.

That he'd messed up. That he still loved me.

I felt my heart swell up with joy when I read that. He still loved me. It was all a mistake.

But I had to resist. I couldn't let him mix me up like that. I'd given him the power to break my heart, and he'd done it.

It had taken him less than a month to prove to me that I'd been right to fear him. To fear his power over me.

All the same, I felt the urge to turn around and drive all the way back to him.

Just to feel his big strong arms around me one more time.

I had felt weak, but he didn't have to know that. In fact, I thought I'd done pretty well for myself. I'd stood up for myself for once.

Plus, telling him off had done one very important thing. After three days, it had finally made me stop crying.

I nodded to Petunia in her cat case and started the car again.

"Gabe Jackson can go right to hell!"

GABE

She was okay.

Tabby was safe. That's what mattered. But I was still shit out of luck.

I stared at the phone in stunned disbelief. I hadn't expected her to fall into my arms and forgive me exactly but I hadn't expected this either!

She had told me off! The sweet, loving woman who'd given me her virginity had actually told me to go to hell.

She'd more or less broken up with me and then gone dark.

And now she was ignoring my texts. True, the way she'd signed off had been adorable. It was typical Tabitha. Worrying and sweet and scolding all at once.

But she'd told me goodbye at the end. Told me to take care. It sounded so final.

Well, I was not having it. Not for one more minute. She was mine dammit! I had screwed up but I apologized. It didn't have to mess up the rest of our lives!

Tabby!
Dammit woman, do not disappear on me like that!
I love you dammit!

I waited but she was gone. I could almost guarantee she had turned the phone off. Well, this was getting me nowhere. I cursed and threw my phone across the room.

I had no idea where she was and that drove me nuts.

Worse than that, I knew she considered herself single. I felt a sickening wave of jealousy come crashing over me. I'd pushed her away and now she was out there, beautiful and vulnerable and alone.

Maybe she was too upset to say no to a handsome stranger who wanted to take care of her.

Maybe another guy would snatch her up, protect her, love her.

Maybe another guy would prove himself worthy.

I held my head in my hands. I had to do something to get her back. I had to at least try and get her to believe that I loved her.

She could be anywhere though.

And I had no way of finding her.

Or did I? I rubbed my eyes. I had been trying to sober up since yesterday and the lack of sleep wasn't helping me think straight.

I had to focus.

I furrowed my brow and realized I had an 'in.' My men. It was hard as hell to get in touch with them when they were at sea, but if they were on base…

I sent out a message request to Hobbs. He was the one who was always hogging the damn lines so I figured he would see it first.

Plus, it was his ass I'd saved when I pushed him down on the deck.

I got a message back about twenty minutes later. We opened a chat window and there he was, just like old times. Even in chat he seemed loud.

Torp!!! What's the good word man?

I wanted to see how you assholes were doing without me.

We cry ourselves to sleep every night.

I bet. How's the ship?

Good as new. Not as shiny without you. No elbow grease. New CO's a lightweight.

I GRINNED. I had been kind of a hard ass about shit like that. It was good to know I was missed.

Can I do anything for you, Torp?

Yeah, I need recon. Can you get me the 411 on a missing person?

Who's missing?

My woman. We had a fight and she took off. I need to find her.

Say no more. You got a general vicinity?

No, just a cell phone. And where she rented a truck.

Hit me up and I'll get back to you at 0:800.

Your time or mine?

Yours.

Thanks man I owe you one.

No way Torp. You took a hit for me. Plus I always thought you had pretty eyes.

I laughed. He really was a cut up.

Tell the guys I say hi.

Will do.

I signed off, wondering why I hadn't done this sooner. I missed the hell out of the crew but we had only talked a handful of times. In a way I'd been running away from the reality of my situation. That I was really out of the service for good.

That I was a different man now. I'd changed. From the accident, sure. But more than that, Tabby had changed me.

Even if I walked again without assistance, I was different. And I was out of uniform for good.

Tabby had made me a man in a way I had never realized was possible. A man who looked after what was his. A protector.

I wanted to be more than an officer now. I wanted to be a husband and hopefully a father.

It was taking some getting used to. But I felt a lightness in my chest. I had missed talking to my crew way too nuch. And they were going to help me find Tabby.

I knew they wouldn't fail me.

I finally crashed for the first time in days.

TABBY

I checked my phone again when I woke up in the dingy motel. The bed was uncomfortable and looked gross, so I slept on top with a towel as a blanket and my jacket balled up under my head.

But I slept, and that's what mattered.

I got myself a cup of coffee in the diner next door and checked my phone.

Gabe had messaged me a few times right after I hung up that morning, but nothing since then. He had told me he loved me though. A couple of times.

I wanted to believe him. But could I? How could he love me, and then not, and then love me again?

I shoved my phone in my purse and got busy loading the van and making sure Petunia was comfortable. She's spent the night in the motel bathroom and was none too happy with me.

But fresh ripped up newspapers in her litter bin and a whole can of turkey and salmon flavored wet food seemed to cheer her up again.

"I promise we'll find a good spot soon. I'll make sure there's a nice big window with lots of birds to look at."

She ignored me, slurping up the canned food like a vacuum. I scratched her head.

"Silly creature."

I turned the ignition and searched for a good radio station. A pop song came on that we used to dance to all the time in high school. Not that I'd ever danced in public, but in Jackie's bedroom it had been a regular night club for two.

I checked the map again and pulled into traffic. I was one day closer to the next phase of my life. Wherever that may be.

"Let's do this."

GABE

abe?"

I heard my mother's voice and opened my eyes. *Shit!* I must have fallen more deeply asleep that I planned. I immediately grabbed my phone to check the time.

Phew, I still had an hour before the rendezvous with Hobbs.

"You alright hon? You slept through the doorbell."

"Yeah, sorry mom."

"There's some things that came for you. I wasn't sure what to do with them."

"What is it?"

"Well, there's this." She handed me an envelope with Tabby's handwriting. "And there's some boxes from Bloomingdales. They have Tabby's name on them."

I felt dread pound in my belly as I opened up the envelope.

The car keys fell out into my hand.

I knew she had rented something to move but I'd hoped she had just attached a rental trailer to the SUV. If she had the car it would mean there was still a chance.

A chance she was thinking about me.

And it only got worse. She'd rejected my gifts as well. They must have arrived just after we had our fight.

I grimaced, imagining how well *that* had gone down.

I stared at the boxes as my mother stacked them by the breakfast bar in the rec room. I would find a way to get them to her. I wanted her to have nice new clothes, even if she hated me.

Even if she wore them for someone else.

I loved her that much. Almost losing her was making it obvious how deep that love went. All the way down to the fucking bedrock.

I'd already knew I was head over heels in love when I ordered all that stuff. Then I'd let some idiot ruin everything. I wanted to smash Josh in the face, and all of his buddies for egging him on.

But I couldn't blame them for everything.

I was the worst offender of all. I knew what a good person Tabby was. I knew she was better than that. Even if she hadn't been a virgin, she wouldn't have cheated on me.

She just wouldn't. I knew it in my gut. I'd always known it.

My jealousy had gotten the best of me. I'd been so afraid that she'd played me. That I'd given her my heart and that she would smash it.

Instead, I'd smashed hers.

I groaned and closed my eyes, closing my fingers over the keys. I wasn't giving the car back to Lyle. I was going to find Tabby and make her take it.

Even if it was just to say goodbye.

My laptop beeped and I perked up. Maybe, just maybe, I'd have a chance to tell her how much I loved her in person.

Maybe she'd believe me.

Maybe she'd take me back.

I opened up the secure link and waited.

TABBY

B*ang bang bang bang!*

I sat up, looking around in confusion. For a minute I didn't know where I was. Then I remembered.

I was in another cheap motel, in another town, in another state.

I'd run away from my problems. Run away from Gabe. I still felt a sharp stab of pain every time I thought of him. And since I was pretty much always thinking about him, that pain was constant.

I'd lost track of how far I'd come. But I was getting a lot closer to a place to land, at least for a little bit.

I was pretty sure I was in North Carolina already… It had been dark when I pulled in. I was looking forward to driving in the sun today.

But it wasn't daylight. It was still dark out. In fact, I had no idea how late it was or how long I'd been asleep.

My hair was in my eyes as I made my way across the room. I was about to open the door when I realized a few things:

1. It was late at night
2. I was a woman alone in the middle of nowhere
3. There was no reason for anyone to be banging on my door

No *good* reason anyway.

I approached the door slowly, tiptoeing so whoever was outside wouldn't hear me. I stood as tall as I could to see out the peephole.

A man stood outside. He was big and tall. And even from the back he looked pissed. He turned and my stomach dropped.

"Gabe?"

His head swiveled towards the door and he leaned both arms against it. He stared at the peephole, a determined look on his achingly handsome face.

"Open the door Tabitha."

I stared in shock at the wild look in his eyes. He looked crazed. He looked desperate.

He looked kinda mean, too.

"What are you doing here, Gabe?"

"Open. The. Door."

I swallowed and put the chain on, trying to gather my thoughts. Then I opened the door a crack. His eyes flared at the sight of me. Then he saw the chain.

He pushed on the door a little.

"Tabby…"

"What do you want?"

"You know what I want Tabby… let me in."

The heat in his gaze was unmistakable. He wanted me. He wanted sex.

I felt an answering thrill in my center. But I couldn't just give in to him. He'd been a real bastard. And if he wanted to use me to get off again, forget it.

It didn't matter how strong our chemistry was. I just had to fight my urges. And his.

"I'm not your blow up toy, Gabe. You can't just throw me away and take me out when you want a little fun."

The muscle in his jaw ticked but he didn't move otherwise.

"I want a lot more than a little fun and you know it."

I stared at him. He stared back.

"Let me in Tabby. You won't like the consequences if you don't."

"Is that a threat?"

He shook his head slowly.

"It's a promise."

I started to shut the door. I was going to let him in, but he didn't know that. He caught the door in his hand.

"I took three taxis, a bus and a plane to get here. You are going to hear me out if nothing else."

Wood shattered with a loud bang as he broke the door in. I stepped back as his massive form filled the doorframe. Then he stepped inside and shut the door.

And locked it.

Before I could even move, he grabbed my car keys off the table and shoved them down the front of his pants. He smiled at me coldly and leaned against the dresser.

"What are you doing, Gabe?"

"I'm done playing games."

"This isn't a game! This is my life."

"No. It's *our* life. Together. Remember? I don't know where the hell you think you are going-"

"I'm going to Florida!" I stomped my foot and he smiled at me like I was a little ball of fluff.

"You're not going to Florida."

"What? Yes, I am. Give me my keys."

He started unbuttoning his shirt, walking towards me.

"Come and get them."

I stared at him as he started stripping. He pulled his shirt off his shoulders and I nearly started drooling at the sight of his chiseled muscles. I knew the things he could do with those arms… with that gorgeous body…

His eyes were dark with sensual promise as he came closer. That's when I noticed it.

"You aren't using your walker."

He shook his head and held up his cane. Then he leaned it against the wall.

"That's right. I made you a promise didn't I?"

My voice was shaky as he got close enough that I could feel the heat coming off his body. He radiated heat and strength and desire. I felt my knees buckle, just from proximity.

"What?"

"I said I was going to take you up against a wall."

"Gabe-"

He growled and caught my hands, pressing them into the small of my back. He held me immobile as he dragged me against him, kissing me deeply. He let his other hand wander, touching every part of me while he murmured his appreciation.

I couldn't think. Or breathe. Or move.

All I could do was feel.

"You're mine Tabby. I'll never let you go."

He gripped me tighter, squeezing my wrists. I whimpered as he guided me towards the wall and then pushed me up against it.

"That's right. I'm going to have you right… here."

He gripped my thighs, pulling them up and over his hips. I felt him grinding himself into me.

"I love you. Tell me you love me."

I moaned as he gripped my top and tore it, exposing my breasts. He lowered his head and kissed my cleavage, his hands cupping my ass.

"Not like this Gabe."

His head snapped up, his eyes practically glowing with heat.

"What not like this?"

"Your leg…"

"My fucking leg is fine." He stared at me, his jaw ticking. "But if you prefer the bed…"

"I do."

He growled and lifted me again, carrying me to the bed. He'd never been like this before. He'd never been this aggressive.

"I missed you." He pulled his perfect cock out of his pants and I stared at it, my mouth watering a little. "*He* missed you."

He knelt on the edge of the bed and grabbed me, tearing my jeans off. I'd slept in my clothes, minus a bra and shoes of course.

That sped up the process quite a bit. That and the sheer brute force Gabe was showing. It was like he was someone else.

Someone who'd been bitten by a werewolf. Or a radioactive bug. Or been turned into a mutant in a lab, set on world domination.

But Gabe just wanted one thing. *Me.*

He shredded my panties and dove between my legs, licking and stroking and sucking my pussy lips. My mind was washed away with the sensations. I let the feelings wash through me, overwhelmed in a good way.

A very, very good way.

In no time, I was rocking my hips against his greedy lips and tongue. He chuckled low and leaned back, his finger making lazy circles on my clit.

"Do you know how fucking scared I've been?"

I was breathing hard, staring at him while he peeled his pants off. He dragged the tip of his cock up and down my slippery pussy lips.

"I've been out of my mind worrying about you."

He pushed inside me. Just a little.

"Never run out on me again. Promise me."

He groaned and slid deeper.

"You're coming back with me."

He grabbed my face and took my mouth in a punishing kiss. I kissed him back just as hard and shook my head.

"No."

He stopped easing into me, staring down at me in shock.

"What?"

"I'm not going back there. Not now. Maybe not ever."

He moaned as his cock twitched, halfway inside me. Neither of us moved.

"Tabby, you have to come back. I told you- I love you. I'm gonna marry you."

I closed my eyes.

"I'm not going back. And as for the rest." I looked up at him. "You haven't asked me yet."

He cursed and started moving again, sliding in a little deeper. "Goddamn it, Tabby. You- oh God- you are mine. Promise me. Say that you belong to me."

I stared at him. I didn't care what he'd done. He was here now, and he loved me. He kept saying so.

And so help me God, I loved him back.

"I promise. I belong to you."
I wrapped my legs around him.
"But I'm not going back."

GABE

The woman beneath me was driving me wild, arching her back. Moving her hips in time with my over eager thrusts. She was different this time.

There was something untamed about her.

And it was making it hard for me to hold my shit together.

I started to lose my tempo. I was too close. I'd waited too long and been too unsure that I'd ever get to hold her this way again.

"Tabby- slow down- I'm gonna-"

She just smiled and lifted her hips. She didn't care that she was ripping me in two. She was refusing to come back with me.

But I couldn't think about that right now. Right now I had to just try not to-

"Ahhhhh!"

I felt my stomach tighten as pleasure ripped through me. All the muscles in my body tensed up and then released as my balls pumped a massive load up my shaft.

Maybe it was the fear. Maybe it was the exhaustion. But I had never come that hard in my life.

I tried to talk but it came out as gibberish. And Tabby wasn't through with me. She was coming too, her legs locked behind me as she milked me for all I was worth.

Which wasn't much without my woman.

And she *was* mine. She'd promised me that. I didn't like anything else she'd said after that though.

That she wasn't leaving with me. That she hadn't decided to marry me yet. And she hadn't said the 'L' word either.

She hadn't admitted she still loved me.

It didn't matter. I wasn't leaving this hotel room without her. Not for food. Not if the sky started falling.

I was in it to win it.

"Jesus Tabby- Oh GOD!"

I didn't think there was anything left but I felt my cock spurt again. It was an aftershock of pleasure so intense I thought I'd died and gone to heaven. I was pretty much a drooling idiot as I collapsed on top of Tabby, her generous curves cushioning my body.

I finally rolled to the side, refusing to release her from my grip. I cradled her against me.

"You're coming with me."

"No, Gabe. I'm not."

I squeezed her and kissed her forehead.

"Fine. You need more convincing. I'm okay with that."

I rolled her onto her back. She stared up at me, her eyes wide.

"Again."

I was still hard and ready for more. And clearly she needed a firm hand to get her under control. I slid my cock into her sweet, warm body. She was soaking wet with our juices.

"I love you."

I pulled out and pushed in again.

"You love me."

I grabbed her leg and pulled it up so it rested on my shoulder. Then I pulled the other leg up too. This way, I could see her perfectly. And my hands were free.

There was so much I could do with my hands…

I grinned at her startled expression.

"You're gonna agree to be my wife by dawn."

"Gabe-"

"Shhhh…"

I reached down and circled my finger over her clit. Her body clenched down on me as I guided her to another orgasm.

"The only words I want to hear from you are 'yes' and 'oh yes'."

She moaned in response and I grinned.

This was going to be fun.

TABBY

TWENTY-FOUR HOURS LATER

"Please Gabe… Oh GOD!"

"Will you marry me?" He was riding me hard but keeping me on the edge. He'd been toying with me for hours. Not just a few either.

Eighteen hours or so.

Basically, since the moment I'd said I wasn't going back with him. It was obvious he wasn't used to taking no for an answer.

And I wasn't used to being played like a grand piano.

Gabe Jackson was very, very good with his fingers.

"Hmmfffff!"

I bit the pillow, my fingers gripping the edge of the mattress. I was covered in a thin sheen of sweat as Gabe drove into me from behind. His fingers danced over my flesh, moving from one sensitive spot to the next.

It felt so good.

Everything he was doing felt good.

Good, but not *satisfying*. He wouldn't let me finish. For almost a full day now, he'd been bringing me to the edge and stopping. He'd even ordered in Chinese food and eaten it while I lay there, begging for release.

He had fed me a little bit, but still, it was cruel. He was being a complete bastard. He pulled out again and I felt him blowing cool air on my pussy. I moaned incoherently.

"Say yes sweetheart and I'll let you come."

I whimpered and tried to bounce backwards on his shaft. He slapped my ass and held me still, not moving. Just the tip was inside me now, making me quiver with the need for more.

More pressure. More fullness. More *him.*

"Okay how about this- say yes and I will take you to a much nicer hotel, marry you and we can go anywhere you want."

"What?"

He slid into me slowly.

"We can go to a nicer hotel."

"Uhhh… after that… what you said after that."

He grunted with each thrust as he punctuated his words with his thick pulsing cock.

"I'm gonna marry you. Unfff."

"Hmmm… oh yes… what else did you say?"

"We can go anywhere. You know that. Unfff."

"Go… for a huh-oh God, yes- honeymoon?"

He flipped me over and grinned at me, sliding back inside me in one fluid motion.

"Yeah, and after too. I don't fucking care where we go. Just say yes."

"Yes."

His eyes got wide and he stopped fucking me for a minute.

"'Yes' you'll marry me?"

"Yes baby, now can you just-"

He flexed his hips, grinning like a mad man.

"You want this?"

"Yes- please Gabe!"

He gave me a look of pure suspicion. I moaned as he pulled halfway out of me.

"But you kept saying no!"

"I said no to going back with you- not to- hmmffff- going forward."

He let out a whoop and kissed me, hard. "We're getting married!" I laughed weakly and tried to get him to focus.

"Don't stop!"

He gave me an evil grin and started fucking me slow and steady.

"Are you gonna be a good girl?"

"Yes, oh God, yes!"

Gabe looked me over while he fucked me, a big grin on his face.

"All this is gonna be mine. Legally."

I murmured 'yes' and he kissed me again, sliding his fingers down to my clit. He strummed it hard and fast.

"Come for me, Tabby."

I screamed as I came. Loud. Gabe kissed me to stifle the sound. It didn't matter. We were going to have to leave this motel after this.

Fast.

I was pretty sure I woke up anyone in a fifty foot radius. In fact, I was vaguely worried in the back of my mind about cops breaking down the door.

"Damn girl!"

I moaned and hitched my hips upward. Gabe's eyes got wide as he felt me squeeze down on him. Hard.

Then he screamed too.

He started thrusting wildly and shouting as I felt him swell up inside me. Then the damn burst and he launched his seed into me, pumping his cock into me again and again.

I just held on tight and shook right along with him.

It was loud. The man sounded like a pissed off walrus. If I hadn't still been coming, I would have laughed.

Oh yeah, we were definitely going to need to get to another hotel.

GABE

"How long will it take you to get here from Paris for your best friend's wedding?"

I was on the balcony of our new hotel suite, whispering on my phone. I didn't think Tabby could hear me, but who could say?

The woman had almost caught me sneaking around with her phone after we'd checked in. I had got what I needed though. The three phone numbers that mattered.

We were getting married dammit. And I wanted her friends there. She deserved everything to be perfect.

Or as perfect as I could make it!

Jackie laughed.

"Please tell me this is Gabe Jackson."

I grinned and stood up straight. Tabby must have told her about me after all. I strutted back and forth with my cane, feeling pleased with myself.

"You approve then?"

"It was you or George Clooney for her. No one else would do."

"George Clooney? The actor?"

I scowled, wondering if I had competition.

"Relax Gabe, he's already married."

I felt the tension go out of my shoulders.

"Oh. So, how soon can you get here? I want everything to be perfect."

"Where is this wedding happening?"

I shrugged.

"I haven't gotten that far yet. Some place warm?"

I glanced into the hotel room to make sure Tabby was still in the bath. I saw the cat, Petunia. She was sitting on the table, daintily cleaning her paws.

I'd had to pay extra to get the damn cat checked in. But Tabby loved the thing. Or her Gran had, so we were keeping it.

I kind of liked the scruffy little thing to be honest.

"Someplace we can bring a cat? Oh and we have all of Tabitha's earthly possessions in a van too."

"Hmmm, so someplace romantic, not a plane ride that we can all get to within a couple of days…"

"That sounds about right."

"I know the perfect place…"

Ten minutes later we had a plan. Jackie was making inquiries and cc'ing my mom on the emails. She'd make sure Dennis and Maryann made it too.

I'd take care of getting Tabby there, even if I had to tie her up. I was still half afraid she'd remember what a jackass I'd been and take off on me again.

"What are you up to?"

Tabitha leaned against the doorway in a fluffy hotel robe. Her hair was damp and curling at the ends. She looked beautiful with her wet hair and freshly scrubbed skin. I realized I'd never seen her fresh out of the shower.

I liked it. I liked it a lot.

I grinned and slid my phone into my pocket.

"Goofing off."

She smiled at me shyly. Little did she know I was planning our life together. I even thought I might have some ideas about where to settle down.

Start a family.

Speaking of which…

I pulled her against me and tugged at the belt of her robe.

"Gabe! I thought you said you were hungry!"

I shook my head and carried her to the bed.

"I thought I'd skip room service and go right for dessert."

She giggled and slipped her arms around my neck.

"Okay."

I lowered her to the bed. I should probably be using my cane, but the rush of having her in my arms kept making me forget. I felt strong, if a little sore, at the end of the long day of driving.

Her lush curves peeked out from the edges of her robe. I licked my lips and opened the robe so I could look my fill at her body. She was so beautiful, and it wasn't just her looks.

She was kind, and real, and strong.

Most of all, she was mine.

I gripped her ankles and spread them wide. Then I kissed the inside of each ankle. Then her calves. She shimmied a little as I got to her knees.

"Hold still young lady!"

Her giggle turned into a squeak as I nipped her inner thigh. I traced the long line of her leg with my tongue, coming almost to the sweet, pouty lips above.

"Hmmm… you look so tasty…"

Her hips wiggled and I grinned, deciding to tease her a little more. I licked and kissed her from her knee to the top of her thighs a couple times again.

"Gabe!"

"Hmm… what? I'm having my dessert. Your leg is very tasty."

"But-"

"But what?" I looked up at her with an innocent look on my face. "Did you want me to do something else?"

She bit her lip, clearly feeling shy. Well, I wanted to hear it. I needed to know she wanted me as bad as I wanted her.

"No but…"

"What is it sweetheart?"

"Can you do it… a little bit higher?"

I laughed and buried my head in my hands. She was so cute and proper. I couldn't imagine a more polite way to ask someone to eat their pussy.

I couldn't stop my shoulders from shaking but I managed to nod.

"Yes, sweetheart. I can do it a little bit higher."

TABBY

"Myrtle Beach?" I frowned at the map, realizing we were backtracking. "What's there?"

"Well, it's close to a few teaching hospitals. And I thought it might be a good spot to open up a place. Plus, there's a base near there."

He smiled at me.

"You know. A good place for both of us to start over. We can take a few days and check it out. Cool?"

"Okay."

I sighed and leaned back, happiness filling my chest. He'd really thought about this. The two of us starting over together. We had hit a rough spot but he'd said he was sorry. And more than that, he'd proved to me he wanted me for good.

Bad enough to chase me halfway down the coast.

Bad enough to go anywhere I wanted to go.

Bad enough that he couldn't keep his hands off me. Or his lips. Or his manly parts.

I blushed a little, remembering last night. We'd checked into a fancy hotel and he'd expanded my sexual education.

By a lot.

Gabe had spent at least an hour between my thighs, bringing me to orgasm again and again with his lips and tongue and fingers. Then we'd made love twice.

And that was just before dinner. He'd kept me up half the night, waking me from short naps to make love again.

This morning he'd taken me slowly, sliding into me from behind before I was fully awake. I'd opened my eyes on the brink of a massive orgasm as he rode me gently, his fingers lightly tweaking my nipples. He'd kept us both on the edge for hours, until we had to rush to check out.

Now we were having our coffee in styrofoam cups on the road. I sighed contentedly. Even Petunia seemed happy that Gabe was here. She'd taken an instant liking to him. Now she was nibbling away on a treat in her cat carrier at my feet.

I wondered what he'd come up with for us to try next.

"Penny for your thoughts." He reached out and squeezed my hand. "What has you smiling like that?"

I blushed and shook my head.

"Nothing. I'm just… happy."

He squeezed my hand again.

"Me too." We were quiet for a while. Then he asked if I wanted to stretch my legs. "Want to stop for lunch soon? We could go for a walk. There's zero rush to get where we're going."

I nodded happily.

"Holler when you see something good."

We pulled off the highway to check out some of the smaller towns along the coast. North Carolina was so pretty, though it was still pretty cold.

Not nearly as cold as Massachusettes though!

I sat up and stared out the window at a cute little town. All the buildings were old, with cheerful Christmas decorations up. It looked like a postcard.

"Oooh, look! A pancake house!"

There was something so cute about the red and white stripped awning and old neon sign. I just knew those pancakes were going to be good. I could use another cup of coffee too, I thought with a yawn.

Gabe found parking and we walked around the town, window shopping. We checked on Petunia again, turning the heat on for a few minutes before we went into the pancake house and sat down.

We both had hot coffee and looked over the menus. Gabe asked me what I was having and I told him I was thinking about waffles.

"Waffles in a pancake house? That's sacrilegious!"

I shook my head, laughing. He was so funny. He seemed lighter now. Maybe its because we were together again. Maybe it was using the cane. Or maybe it was just us each getting a chance to start fresh.

I think it was probably all three. I knew because I felt it too.

Gabe's phone beeped. He ignored it until I told him he could answer it. I knew he was just being polite. He smiled sheepishly after he checked his text.

"My mom. Can I send her a picture?"

I nodded and he scooted over to my side of the table. He held up the phone and took some shots, scrolling through them.

"Damn, you're beautiful. Have I told you that lately?"

"Only about a hundred times today."

He kissed my cheek and slid back to his side of the table.

To think that a few days ago I was crying my eyes out and now I was sending selfies to my future mother-in-law… well, it was kind of amazing.

It was a miracle.

"I might send this to the guys too. I owe them one."

"For what?"
He smiled at me.
"For helping me find you."

GABE

"Did you find a dress?"

"Yes, I- whoops!"

Jackie stopped mid-sentence and jumped behind a column. We were on the veranda of the place we were all staying at.

Of course, Tabby didn't know any of this. Which is why Jackie was hiding. I grinned at the spritely little woman. She had a sharp black bob, multiple ear piercings and was wearing head to toe black. She was sort of a grown up goth.

We hadn't talked once in high school but boy was I glad to be talking to her now. Plus, she clearly loved Tabby to pieces, so we already had that in common.

Yeah, Jackie was saving my ass.

The hotel she'd found was amazing. Small and charming with a restaurant on the water.

And they were happy to accommodate a last minute wedding.

Thank God it was the off season.

"Sorry, thought I saw her."

I smiled to myself. I knew Tabby was passed out. I'd given her another orgasm in the shower as soon as we'd checked in. I would wake her up for dinner, but considering how much sex time we'd been getting in, she needed her sleep.

I wanted her rested. She had to be with what I had in mind.

"She's sleeping. I tucked her in myself."

"You are so domesticated. I never would have guessed."

Jackie was smiling at me like I was a cute little puppy dog. I shrugged. It was true. Tabby had domesticated me, without even trying.

"You aren't going to hurt her again are you? Because I'll have to kill you."

I raised my hands. I had a feeling she could do it too. Sort of sneak up on me with a weapon, like a tiny ninja.

"Never. I swear."

She gave me an assessing look and I realized why they were friends. Jackie was no dummie. Even though she looked uber fashionable and hard edged compared to my girl, they were two peas in a pod.

And Tabby was stylish in her way. She just used that style to try and hide her ridiculously slammin' bod.

I grinned, wondering if the boxes had arrived yet. My mom had sent them ahead. She was getting in tomorrow morning.

Just in time for the rehearsal dinner.

I wanted a surprise wedding, but I'd settled for an almost-surprise wedding. I didn't want Tabby to miss out on any of the fun wedding stuff I'd planned. Or the girly stuff brides liked to do.

After all, she was only getting married once.

My mom was bringing my dress uniform and my grandparent's wedding rings. She'd also picked up the engagement ring I'd already settled on. I hadn't bought it the first time I looked but the jeweler had been more than happy to accept payment over the phone.

Lyle and Topher were coming. And a few of my mom's friends were flying down for the ceremony too.

I'd even found a judge to do the deed.

Now all I needed was to keep it a secret until the rehearsal dinner tomorrow night.

Basically, I needed to keep my woman in bed, screaming in pleasure. Plus, the suite had a nice big bathtub and a walk-in shower. And a soft rug in front of a gas fireplace.

Lots of places for me to teach her some new tricks. Tabby was a fast learner though, so I knew I was going to have to get creative to impress her.

I grinned to myself.

Yeah, pretty sure I could handle that.

TABBY

"What is all this?"

Gabe stood proudly with his cane next to a pile of boxes. He looked so pleased with himself, I didn't have the heart to yell at him. And it was amazing to see him standing there on two legs.

"This is for you. I got it for you before- well, before you left."

"Gabe! I sent that stuff back!"

He shrugged.

"You're starting over in a new town. You need new stuff."

He grinned and raised one eyebrow. He looked positively devilsh. I knew immediately he was up to no good.

"I can make you try it all on. Or you can do it willingly."

"Make me?"

He smiled wider as there was a knock on the door. He opened it and two men in uniform brought something in. I watched in awe as they pushed in a huge rolling tray, piled high with food.

There was a fruit plate, muffins, a thermos of coffee and three jugs of juice. There was a pasta dish, for me I assumed, and a steak and potato for him. Two side salads and something else covered with a napkin in a bowl.

Oh, and a bottle of fancy champagne in a bucket of ice with two fluted glasses.

"Why did you get so much food?"

"Because I knew we wouldn't be leaving the room until tomorrow."

My eyes got wide.

"Oh. So we're staying in then."

He laughed and tugged the napkin off the deep bowl in the center. Two huge cans of whipped cream were inside. My mouth went dry.

"I was expecting bread and butter."

He smiled and started shaking one of the cans.

"Do you want your dinner hot? Or cold?"

I knew what he was asking. If I wanted to eat. Or… be eaten. I chose the later.

"Cold. Definitely cold."

He grinned wickedly and grabbed me.

"My thoughts exactly."

Then he sprayed whipped cream down the front of my shirt.

"Gabe!"

"Relax sweetheart. I'm going to make sure you get clean." He nuzzled my neck, licking some of the whipped cream right out of my cleavage.

"And after, I'll wash you again just to make sure you're not sticky. We are going to make use of the big shower." I stared at him, realization dawning. "Especially the bench."

I WOKE up in the early afternoon. I moaned and rolled over, every inch of my body feeling deliciously heavy. Thankfully, I wasn't sore.

Or sticky.

That was particularly impressive considering how much whipped cream had covered my body just a few hours before.

I'd been shocked at what he did with the first bottle. But even more shocked that he'd done it again with the second. He'd gobbled all that sweet stuff off every inch of my body.

Literally every inch.

I had sensitive spots I hadn't even known about. Lots of them. And he'd made use of every one, taunting me with his lips and tongue and fingers for hours.

Yeah… Gabe had an early morning breakfast. Me.

"Wake up sleepyhead."

"Hmmm?"

"I got you some coffee. And here, you didn't try this one on but I think it will work."

He held up a dress on a hanger. It was floaty layers of silk in two shades of purple, one dark and one almost a pale lavender. The fluttery sleeves and shoulder straps were just enough to cover the straps of one of my new bras.

Oh yeah, I had a whole new wardrobe. One that didn't hide my curves, but accentuated them. And weirdly, I didn't feel self-conscious in any of the new clothes.

Gabe had already tricked me into accepting all the stuff he'd gotten. He'd made me a deal when I was slightly less than coherent.

I accepted one box of clothes for each orgasm he gave me.

There were eight boxes and I'd said 'yes' to every one of them.

"Oh. Are we going out? I thought we should start looking for apartments online."

He nodded slowly.

"Yes, we are going out to eat. I want to show you off."

I blushed and smiled at him. For some reason, I liked how possessive and proud he was.

"And don't worry about finding a place, I've been looking at houses instead. Is that okay?"

"Houses? To rent?"

He shrugged. "Maybe."

He sat on the edge of the bed and handed me a coffee. I sipped it while he kissed my bare shoulder, sliding his hand down my back to my hip.

"Hmmmm, if you don't get up soon, we're going to end up staying *in*."

I giggled and scooted off the bed. I was pretty clean but I took a shower just to make sure. Whipped cream got in the darnedest of places, and I was pretty sure my eyebrows were a little sticky.

That was probably the one spot he hadn't licked dry.

I put on the dress and was surprised to find a pretty pair of pumps in a silvery patent leather waiting by the bathroom door. There was even a taupe evening bag with enough room for my phone and a lipstick.

Who knew my boyfriend was so fashion conscious?

I got dressed and combed my hair, patting it dry with a towel. I even put on a little makeup. I nodded at my reflection. There, that was definitely an improvement.

Gabe's face was priceless when I walked out of the bathroom.

"Tabby… you look…"

I giggled and gave him a little twirl.

"Do you like it?"

His mouth opened and shut. I guessed he did like it, judging from the look in his eyes.

"I've never- you never-"

I smiled at him and slid my arms around his neck.

"I've never what?"

"You never wore a dress before!" He blurted it out and I laughed. "You're so beautiful!"

Then he frowned.

"I don't like it."

"You don't?"

"No. You are going to start a damn riot. You are way too pretty and-"

"Only you think that." I kissed him. "But I'm glad you do."

And I was. For the first time in my life, I enjoyed male attention. As long as it was from him.

He grumbled and draped a soft cashmere shawl over my shoulders. I was smiling as he led me downstairs to the hotel's small restaurant. Then I was not smiling.

I was in shock.

Maryann was here. And Dennis and- oh my goodness, Jackie was here all the way from Paris!

I looked at Gabe in wonder.

"Gabe? What did you do?"

He pulled me into his arms and kissed me tenderly.

"Surprise!" He nuzzled his mouth to my ear and whispered. "They're here for the wedding."

"The- what?"

I stared in shock as Gabe slowly lowered himself to his knee. He pulled out a box. He opened it and I saw a beautiful ring. It was a simple gold band with a sparkling diamond in the center.

"I love you Tabitha Peterson. Will you do me the honor of becoming my wife?"

I nodded slowly, realizing my hands were over my face. I lowered them and smiled at him tremulously.

"Yes. Oh my God, yes!"

He grimaced a bit as he used the cane to stand up again. Then he kissed me and the crowd went wild.

I pushed on his shoulder.

"Is your leg okay?"

He nodded and gave me a rueful smile.

"Yeah, I think so. But I won't be doing that again for a while."

I raised an eyebrow.

"Proposing marriage? I should hope not!"

He laughed and kissed me again.

"Don't worry about that. You're the only girl for me, Tabby. I love you so much."

My eyes were full of tears as I stared at his handsome face.

"I love you too."

He grinned and squeezed my hand.

"Come on. My mom wants to congratulate us."

"Your mom is here too?" He nodded and I linked my arm in his. He'd thought of everything. He'd done all of this.

For me.

I smiled so wide it almost hurt.

I was getting married.

GABE

That dress. I moaned to myself. Why did I buy her that dress?

Or the form fitting shirts and skirt and jeans…

She was even more stunningly beautiful than I'd realized. Tabby rivaled the hollywood starlets you saw on magazine covers. But those starlets didn't have her sinful curves.

I was going to spend the rest of my life beating off men with a stick.

A big stick.

I bounced up and down on my heels then resumed pacing, trying it with the cane and without. I was practicing, to see if I could walk down the aisle without assistance.

Though I thought I might bring it anyway. Tabby said it made me look dignified. The guys said it made me look like a bad ass.

Either one sounded pretty good to me.

Topher and Lyle watched me from the other side of the room. They'd abducted me from our hotel room this morning and dragged me to theirs. Thankfully, they'd had my uniform handy and lots of coffee.

Maybe too much coffee. I was climbing the damn walls. I hadn't wanted to leave Tabby alone either. But they'd all ganged up on me. Jackie and Maryann too.

The girls had showed up early to get Tabby ready. They'd started squawking like birds when they saw me still in the suite.

Something about bad luck to see the bride on the wedding day. What they didn't know was, I'd hadn't just seen her.

I'd seen her puke.

I had a feeling that she was either nervous as hell about my semi-surprise wedding or she was pregnant.

I was praying for option two.

"Hey G-Man you are making me dizzy."

"Shut up, man. He's just nervous" Topher punched Lyle's shoulder. "Gabe, we're supposed to tell you to turn on your laptop in five minutes."

He glanced at his watch.

"Four actually."

I glared at them and went to get my bag. I pulled out the laptop and set it up on the desk, searching for the hotel's wifi. I leaned against the desk, too nervous to sit down.

Blooooop.

I knew that sound. It was a secure line. I grinned as the entire crew came into view.

"TORP!"

I grinned at the screen, my nerves momentarily forgotten.

"How are you guys?"

"Top secret, Torp. No can tell."

"SHOW US THE BRIDE!"

Donnelly was goofing off, waving his ass at the computer. I pulled up a photo of Tabby on my phone and held it up to the screen. They went nuts, as expected. I laughed, waiting for the whistling and hooting and hollering to calm down.

"How'd you land her? Holy hell!"

"Can I have one? I'll take a hit if I can get one!"

"Dry land! I want dry land!"

Lyle tapped my shoulder after a few minutes of joking around with my crew. They looked good. It warmed my heart to see them all safe and sound and smiling.

"Uh, Gabe, I think they're ready."

The guys waved goodbye, still commenting on my bride and her tatas. Dave shouted to lay pipe and Donnelly told me to knock her up.

"Impregnation on the wedding night is a longstanding tradition!"

I laughed, thinking it was a good thing Tabby couldn't hear them chanting 'breed her' over and over again. She would not be amused. But hell, it was kind of funny.

I signed off and checked the bathroom mirror. I gargled with mouthwash and gave myself the nod. I looked damn good, if I did say so myself.

"Let's do this."

I followed the guys down the stairs to the lower level. Lyle went ahead to make sure I wouldn't accidentally bump into the bride. When he told me the coast was clear I walked in and shook hands with the judge. Lyle took my cane and stood beside me. Topher had the rings.

I had two best men. And hell, that was just fine.

My mom was beaming at me from the first row as the music started.

It was time.

I was getting married.

The doors opened and Tabitha took one step into the room. Everything stopped. The music seemed to pause. No one spoke. I was pretty sure the world stopped turning.

I *definitely* stopped breathing.

She was stunning in a simple long white dress. It had short cap sleeves and was relatively modest up top, but her curves were still on display. It skimmed softly over her cleavage and the indent of her waist, then out over the gentle swell of her delicious hips.

She stood straight and proud as she walked towards me. She was perfection. Her hair was long and subtly curled, her pink lips were smiling, her gorgeous golden eyes shone brightly with love.

This must be heaven. Because I was surely marrying an angel.

A series of images flashed through my mind. Tabby when we were just kids in junior high. Tabby in high school. Our eyes meeting time and time again.

She'd always looked away first. But this time, she held my eyes proudly. For all to see.

It was really happening.

The most beautiful girl in the world was about to become my wife.

TABBY

My stomach rolled uneasily as I walked down the aisle. Gabe looked so handsome, standing there in his crisp dress uniform. He stood sure and proud on two feet.

The look on his face was almost comical. He looked like he was seeing a mirage. His eyes travelled down my body and back up again. He looked absolutely stunned.

Well, it *was* only the second time he'd seen me in a dress.

He looked kind of relieved to see me too. For a minute, I wondered if he had thought I was going to run out on him again. My heart melted at the thought.

I knew he didn't want to leave me this morning.

As magical as this moment was, I would be relieved if I made it through the ceremony without vomiting. Like I'd been doing all freaking day.

Don't throw up. Don't throw up. Don't throw up.

I'd pretty much been a puke machine since I woke up. In between getting fitted into my dress, getting my hair done, sipping weak tea and oh yeah, dry heaving.

But I was smiling all the same.

The reason why was wrapped in a paper towel, sitting in the hotel bathroom.

A pregnancy test.

And it was positive.

The judge kept the ceremony short and sweet. He spoke about the sanctity of marriage and the love he could see between us. I blushed as Gabe said his vows loud and true. I raised my voice when it was my turn.

Then it was over.

"I now pronounce you man and wife."

Just like that. We were married.

"You may kiss the bride."

Gabe's eyes were hungry and he pulled me close and cupped my face. Then he lowered his face to mine and our lips met. Our first kiss as man and wife. It was lingering and sweet and tender.

Then he squeezed my bottom and I jumped.

"Gabe!"

He grinned at me.

"What? No one noticed that."

I was giggling as we walked down the aisle together and outside to take the wedding photos. Someone handed me a glass of champagne. I handed it to Gabe and he downed it.

Our little party took off at full swing. We talked with the guests as people danced a little and ate and drank. Then we all sat down for a meal.

Jackie and Lyle stood up to make their toasts. Lyle went first.

"Gabe has always been the sort of person who looked out for his buddies. He's a stand up guy and I'm so happy that Tabitha finally gave him the time of day. He only waited ten years to seal the deal." He winked. "I said he was reliable, not fast." Everyone laughed. "My congratulations to the happy couple."

Gabe clapped louder than anyone else.

Then it was Jackie's turn. She held up her glass and I waited, suddenly nervous.

"Tabitha is one of the best people I know. She's always been there for me, no matter what. And now I'm so glad she has someone there for her too."

Everyone applauded. And then Jackie said something that made me cover my face in embarrassment.

"Oh and Gabe, she always had a crush on you too."

Gabe grinned and pulled me in to kiss my neck. I couldn't even look at him. I felt like that same sixteen year old girl, pining for the star football player.

Except that now, I got to go home with him. Wherever that home may be.

Not long after the cake we snuck away. Jackie and Lyle were at the bar, flirting. It was almost comical to see them together. He was a big lug and she was a tiny little thing. But I had to admit, there was something about it that worked.

Gabe carried me over the threshold into our suite. He reached for me, trying to give me a kiss. I waved him off and pulled out my surprise.

Gabe's eyes were wide as I unfolded the paper towel. The little blue plus sign was unmistakable. He stared at my hand, then back at my face, then back at my hand.

"Is that what I think it is?"

I nodded and his face broke out into the biggest smile I'd ever seen on the man. He was usually somewhat reserved, but now he was almost giddy.

He picked me up and spun me around, kissing me soundly.

As soon as he put me down again though, I covered my mouth.

"Oh no. Should I not have done that?"

I was so dizzy, I felt like I might tip over. He grabbed my arm to steady me.

"Are you okay?"

I ran into the bathroom and threw up. It's a good thing I hadn't eaten much at the party. I rinsed my mouth out and pressed my cool hands to my face.

"Tabby?"

"I'm okay. It comes on real fast and then it passes just as quickly."

"So, no roller coaster rides."

"Probably not."

He started peeling off his clothes.

"You just relax baby. We'll get some ginger ale and I'll be real gentle."

"Gentle?"

He smiled and slipped his hands under my dress.

"It's bad luck not to do it on your wedding night."

My eyes got wide as he led me back into the bedroom. The bed was covered in rose petals. He went to the bar and came back with a cup of ginger ale. I sipped it gratefully.

"You sure you are okay, sweetheart?"

"I'm okay."

He guided me down onto the flowers.

He lied about one thing though.

He wasn't gentle.

SEVEN MONTHS LATER

GABE

"Hold on baby! You can do it!"

Tabby was breathing hard and clutching my hand. She was magnificent, somehow managing to look beautiful in a hospital gown. Maybe it was the way the sweat glistened on her flawless skin. Or how her hair was curling around her beautiful face from the effort.

We'd done the classes. We'd babyproofed the house and painted the nursery a pale green. We were ready.

Tabitha had even sewn dresses and dolls and blankets out of soft fabrics in a rainbow of colors.

All while attending nursing school.

She was pretty much a superhero.

Not to mention how good she was at handling me, which wasn't easy. I knew I was pretty demanding. I wanted her attention, and I wanted her close enough to touch.

I touched her a lot.

And I hated it when she was gone for too long.

As a result, I'd started picking her up and dropping her off from her classes. I'd reasoned that it saved gas, even though the Surf Shack was nowhere near her school.

Yeah, I'd finally opened up my little seafood joint. It was still new but so far it was a resounding success. All the other places were either greasy or fancy. Mine was right in that sweet spot in the middle.

I didn't care that it was out of the way though. I'd seen the way the other students looked at her. And the professors. And the doctors she trained with. There was no way in hell I wasn't going to make sure my stamp was seen far and wide.

Basically, I peed in a circle around her every chance I got.

Plus, I drove faster which got her home faster which got us into bed faster.

It was win/win.

And now she was giving me the ultimate gift. A child.

Our child.

"Push!"

She squinched up her gorgeous face as she bore down. Then I saw it. The baby was crowning.

Holy hell. There it was.

I watched in amazement as Tabby pushed and pushed. I held her hand and cheered her on as she managed to get that baby out of her tiny body. She might be small but she was strong as hell. I had to admit, I was impressed.

She barely made a peep.

Our daughter on the other hand had a massive set of lungs on her.

"WAHHHHHHHHHHH!"

The nurse was smiling as she wiped the squalling baby and handed her to my wife. Tabby's face was lit up with joy as she looked from the baby and up to me. She'd never looked more lovely to me. And that was saying something.

I pressed a kiss to her forehead. We sat there quietly, staring at our little bundle of joy.

"Thank you my love."

TABBY

THE HOSPITAL WAS quiet as the nurse handed me the baby for her fist feeding. She was so beautiful, so perfect, she made my heart sing. Her little face puckered and I knew she was about to let out a wail.

I tugged the gown away to offer her my nipple. And just like that, she quieted and latched on. Well, that was easy.

"Wow. That is the sexiest thing I have seen in my whole damn life."

I rolled my eyes at Gabe as he leaned in to get a closer look. He reached out to stroke my other breast with his hand.

"Can I have the other one?"

I laughed and shooed him away.

"Seriously though sweetheart, you look beautiful."

I leaned back and smiled at him. I never got tired of hearing that. Especially when it was so clear that he meant it.

"Thank you."

He reached out and squeezed my hand where I held the baby to my breast.

"How you do feel?"

I smiled at him.

"Like a mama. How do you feel?"

His eyes were a little watery as he gazed at us. There was no mistaking the love shining in his eyes.

"Like the luckiest man in the world."

ABOUT THE AUTHOR

Thank you for reading *Torpedo*! If you enjoyed this book please let me know on by reviewing and on and Goodreads! You can find me on Facebook, Twitter, or you can email me at: JoannaBlakeRomance@gmail.com

Sign up for my newsletter!

Credits:

LJ Anderson, Mayhem Cover Design

Furious Fotog, Cover Photo

Rachael Balted and BT Urreala, Cover Models

Just One More Page Book Promotions

Pincushion Press

Other works by Joanna Blake:

BRO'

A Bad Boy For Summer

PLAYER

PUSH

GRIND (Man Candy Trilogy Book One)

HEAT (Man Candy Trilogy Book Two)

DEEP (Man Candy Trilogy Book Three with extended epilogues)

Go Long

Go Big

Cockpit

Hot Shot

Stud Farm (The Complete Delancey Brothers Collection)

Torpedo

Cuffed

Wanted By The Devil (Devil's Riders Book One)

COMING SOON:

The Continuation of Mason and Cain's stories

The completely rewritten expanded Devil's Riders Trilogy

Turn the page for excerpts from Joanna Blake's *Cuffed, Cockpit, Go Long, GRIND, BRO' and A Bad Boy For Summer.*

I rubbed my cheek where she'd slapped it, admiring the way she looked in those tight jeans of hers as she stomped off. She was a redhead alright. Only a russet haired woman would slap a man after kissing the hell out of him.

And Jenny was one hell of a kisser.

I took my time coming back in. Not because I was worried she'd slap me again. I was just deep in thought.

Mostly thinking about gettin' deep in her.

I sat down and ordered a watered down pitcher of beer. I had a long night ahead of me. I had someone to walk home.

Jenny scowled at me while she took my order, and scowled when she watched the other bartender bring it back. She scowled when she brought me a basket of fries.

The woman basically scowled up and down the whole night.

I sat back and waited for her shift to end, enjoying the memory of the way her luscious body had melted against me. It was getting close to time when she asked me if I wanted anything else. I took my time, staring up and down her body.

"Oh yeah honey, I can think of a lot of things."

"I'm not a piece of meat, Jagger!"

"No, you're definitely not a piece of meat. But you do look tender."

Jenny threw my check at me and turned tail to see to her other tables. I made my last beer count, sipping it slow as molasses until I was the last guy in the place. She started getting ready to close up. She 'accidentally' mopped right over my boots.

I smiled and stood up, throwing a fifty-dollar tip on the table. Her eyes widened. She stared at me as I walked out of the bar.

'Course I was waiting out front for her when she came out fifteen minutes later.

She stared at me. I stared at her. Then she walked up to me and tossed that fifty-dollar bill in my face.

"I'm not for sale you sonofabitch!"

I looked right at her. She was angry. But she had mistaken my meaning.

"I didn't say you were."

"Then what are you doing tipping like that?"

"I took up a seat in your section all night. Seemed fair."

She stared at me belligerently.

"Well, I'm not taking it."

"How about a twenty?"

"What are you, a cash machine?"

She huffed, crossing her arms over her chest. Her glorious, perfect, mind-bending chest. I pulled out a ten and a five.

"Fifteen?"

She yanked the money out of my hand so fast I got rug burn. Then she stomped off. The woman had a pair of legs on her. And she made good use of them.

I was whistling as I followed her back towards the base.

GRIND

Something wet slid against my ear. I brushed it away, still half asleep. It grazed my skin again and I rolled away from it. I tried to wipe it off on the pillow beneath my head, grimacing at the slimy sensation. Now I was awake and I didn't want to be.

Damn.

I opened my eyes to see a woman bending over me. Her long blond hair brushed my face. I turned my head away.

"Cut it out."

She sat up, glaring at me.

"You didn't seem to mind last night."

Normally, I would have soothed her. Called her by name. Trouble is, I had no fucking clue who the hell she was.

I looked around.

I had no idea *where* I was either.

"Fuck me."

She grinned at me, tossing that long bleached hair over her shoulder.

"I already did."

Belatedly I noticed that she was wearing some serious lingerie. Black and cream lace. It matched her bedroom. Her very expensive looking bedroom.

I was swimming in a sea of neutral toned sheets and blankets. Silk probably. Expensive, definitely.

"I'd like to again."

I shook my head.

"Sorry babe, I gotta go."

She pouted. I rolled out of bed, looking for my clothes.

"Oh come on... Didn't we have fun together last night?"

I smiled and nodded. It's not that she was bad looking, even if she was at least a decade older than me. It was hard to tell with these rich older broads. She was toned, buffed and polished to a high shine.

Well preserved didn't even begin to cover it.

Yeah, she was hot. Not just for a cougar. But I wasn't in the mood. I didn't usually go for seconds anyway.

Hell. I never did.

Hit it and quit it was my motto. It served me well. I didn't want any entanglements and I doubted I ever would.

I looked at her, giving my best impersonation of someone who gave a shit.

"Where are my clothes?"

She smiled back and shrugged.

"I really couldn't say."

Fucking hell.

"That's great. Just great."

I looked around the room, lifting cushions and opening drawers. Nada. On the bedside table were my keys, wallet and phone. I scooped them up, thanking God for small favors.

"Have a nice day, Ma'am."

"Wait- you aren't leaving like that!"

I coyly waved bye bye to her and left. I jogged through her palatial house in the buff. The marble floors were cool under my feet. The place screamed mega bucks. But not in a tacky way. It was tastefully done, just like the lady herself.

She was chasing me through the house, becoming less composed by the second.

"Seriously, you can't! What will the neighbors think?"

I stopped at the front door of her mansion, glancing back over my shoulder.

"You should have thought of that before you hid my shit."

She screamed in frustration and threw a vase at me. I heard it shatter against the door as I closed it behind me. Just in the nick of time.

"Damn. That would have left a mark."

I made a call as I strolled down her manicured driveway to the gate.

"Joss, can you pick me up? I need a ride."

I leaned against the wrought iron gate and waved at a neighbor who was walking their dog.

"Take your time."

Not one for slacking I started my first full day home with a match against the club pro Matt. It cost extra to play with him but I didn't care. He was an amazing player and gave as good as he got. And for some reason, he considered me a friend.

Probably because most of the people who hired him were bored housewives hoping to get into his pants.

I'd noticed the cougar crowd dropping me hints the past few years as well. And now that I was 21... well maybe I'd take one of them up on it. At least I could be sure an older woman would know what she was doing.

I was dripping with sweat by the time we were done. I wasn't a big fan of showering at the club so I left. Matt waved me off and begged me to book him as much as possible this summer. I promised I would.

What the fuck else was I supposed to do?

Except, well, fuck.

As much as possible.

As many girls as possible.

Speaking of which maybe I'd text Jen later. I knew she was waiting on me. I did enjoy working out horizontally, especially with a sexy female like Jen. She liked to sport fuck as much as I did.

I was turning down our driveway in my convertible when I hit the breaks.

Hard.

A girl was biking toward me. From the general direction of the house. Long dark blond hair blew behind. Big high tits filled out her t-shirt admirably. She had a teeny tiny waist and long tanned legs. She rode closer and I tried to get a look at her face.

Pretty, that much was obvious, with big beautiful eyes. I could see her puffy lips from twenty feet away. Cute little nose too.

The girl looked like a God damned swimsuit model.

No. Wait. What.

My brain went utterly blank as I realized something.

It was Mouse. Mouse was the swim suit model. I was staring at Mouse with lust.

Hot, unrelenting lust.

I jolted to action as she pulled up by my car.

"Nev?"

She stopped her bike, those impossibly long legs straddling the seat. Her jean shorts were short, almost up to the top of her perfect thighs. I swallowed, realizing my mouth was a little bit dry.

But my dick was throbbing.

She smiled at me, cool as a cucumber. Where was the worshipful little Mouse I knew and loved?

"Hey Clay."

She'd grown up obviously. And she'd grown up right.

Still, I knew how to charm the pants off a girl, no matter how hot she was. And I wanted to. I knew it instantly. I wanted to fuck Mouse, of all people.

Really, really bad.

I smiled, letting my eyes wander over that ridiculously perfect little body.

"Where you going?"

She tossed her head, sending a cascade of wavy blond hair over her shoulder. It was very sexy, but not deliberate or coy. She was unconsciously seductive. It was hypnotizing.

"Job hunting."

I smirked.

"In that outfit?"

She looked down at herself and back at me.

I pulled my sunglasses down and switched gears.

"I think you've outgrown those shorts little Mouse."

Then I drove away. Slowly. Very slowly.

Just so I could check out her ass in the rear view window.

Good lord, the girl was fine. She'd stop traffic anywhere. No matter what she was wearing.

I went into the house to change, all thoughts of texting Jen forgotten.

I threw my arm over the back of the seat and looked to the side, letting my eyes slide over her body. Frannie didn't seem to notice. Her hands were gripping the bar that had locked us into place in the Ferris wheel seat.

I leaned back and watched her as the ride started to spin.

She looked like a little kid, nervous and excited. Her cheeks were pink and her eyes sparkled when she turned to look at me.

"I thought you didn't like Ferris wheels."

"I don't! I'm petrified."

I grinned at her.

"I'll protect you."

She laughed as if that were the wittiest thing I could have said. I laughed too, her laughter was that infectious. As soon as we got to the top of the wheel I slid over to her. Her face was startled as she looked into my eyes. My eyes lowered to her soft inviting lips.

I leaned in and tilted my head, angling my mouth against hers.

Her lips felt like pillows underneath mine. Warm and sweet. Her breath mingled with mine as I slowly eased into the kiss, nibbling and licking her until she opened her mouth.

Then the kiss went wild.

My hands reached for her hips as I pulled her against me. Her breasts mashed against my chest and I moaned, diving back into her mouth to tangle my tongue with hers.

I felt like my dick was a fucking rocket, it was so ready to lift off.

The next thing I knew the ride had stopped and a crowd of people were staring at us. I guess we didn't notice. I wanted the ride to go on and on. As it was I had to hold my jacket in front of me as I climbed out.

I glanced at Frannie. Her pretty lips were swollen and pouting. I wanted to get horizontal with her right fucking now.

Jesus Christ, what was she doing to me?

The girl had the moves that was for fucking sure.

I took her hand and pulled her toward the boardwalk, desperately looking for a place to be alone with her. She smiled at me shyly. There was an innocence in her gaze that made me absolutely sure that she had no fucking clue what I had in mind.

I had a sinking feeling that Frannie was a good girl. That her innocence might be a problem. That it might take more than a Ferris wheel ride to get into her pants. It wasn't going to stop me from trying though.

I knew something else too.

I knew it without a doubt.

This girl was going to be mine.

Made in the USA
Columbia, SC
09 July 2017